Second Chances

A Novel

Ben,
May God bless you always!
You're awesome!
Brad

By

Brad Duncan

First Printing, 2015

Bradleyjeep Publishing
ISBN # 978-0-9912858-3-9

Books may be purchased in quantity and/or special sales by contacting
www.3tChallenge.com

Acknowledgements

It's always amazing to see how God can take ordinary people and accomplish extraordinary things. I'm humbled and thrilled by the testimonies I've received from my debut novel, First Fruits. I'm hoping and praying Jesus will use Second Chances to further His Kingdom as well. I'd like to thank Jordan Mountjoy for the cover art; Becky Cummins, Susan Washington, Crissy McEntire, and Madison McEntire for the editing; and Larry Small for the Discussion Questions.

My parents, Ronnie and Linda Duncan, are still in shock that I wrote a book. They are the best parents I can imagine. I appreciate the encouragement from my sister, Jamie, and her husband, Jason Burnside. My girls Maddie, Mackenzie, and Abby are fantastic, and I'm proud to be their dad. They've taught me what it means to "pray continually!" My awesome wife, Michelle, deserves as much credit for this book as I do. I'm blessed to have her in my life and I love her like crazy!

May God bless you on your journey through this life. Any and all glory from this book goes to the Lord Jesus Christ who loves you more than you can imagine! He truly is a God of second chances.

Chapter 1

Pastor Victor Martinez looked across New Hope Church on this Sunday morning and was excited to see so many new believers. His wife, Maria, was sitting with his cousin Hector and his wife Elizabeth Gonzales. Seated on the other side of Maria was Sofia Lopez. She was a young Hispanic mom whose husband, Gabriel, was serving in the military in Afghanistan. Since his deployment, New Hope Church, and especially Maria, had cared for Sofia and her baby. He was born six months after Gabriel was deployed.

The New Hope worship team had just finished the invitation music. Dewayne and Theresa were teenagers on the worship team. They also helped with New Hope's after-school program. Julius, an African American teenager who had recently been saved at the New Hope Church revival, was sitting with his mom, Wanda Williams.

Reginald Dupree was in his mid-forties and he loved his new church home. He had moved to Westside just a few months ago. After visiting with Pastor Victor, he joined New Hope Church and offered to begin a recovery program at the church. He had led a similar program at his previous church. Professionally, Reginald was a pharmacist, so he was familiar with how creative and deceptive addicts can be. His love for God placed a burden upon him to help free these people from the prison of addiction. Alcohol and drugs had destroyed many people in Reginald's life. His wife had been killed five years ago by a drunk driver. This morning he was praising God for the success Julius was having overcoming his addictions. Julius was doing very well in the program.

Pastor Victor said, "It's been a wonderful morning worshiping with all of you. Julius Williams will be one of the many people being baptized next week. He has a word to share before we dismiss. Julius, will you please come forward?"

Julius made his way to the front of the church. He looked out at the members of his church, "Thank you for allowing me a moment to speak. I'm a new believer, but I want you to know I will do my best to make you proud. I'm grateful for you accepting me and helping me grow in my faith. I especially want to thank my mom for loving me and sacrificing for me. Pastor Vic and Brother Reginald, I appreciate both of you for spending so much time and energy teaching me about God. I'm doing my best to make up for my mistakes and follow the Lord. I love this church, and I love my Jesus."

Julius sat down and Victor stepped back up, "Thank you, Julius. I am very proud of the man you are becoming. Let's keep our friends at Big Oak Christian Church and their pastor, Patrick Spakes, in our prayers. He's still taking some time off due to his son Daniel's passing a few weeks ago.

"Brother Reginald will be leading our recovery program tomorrow night. I'm so proud of all of you who are fighting the good fight to stay sober. The Lord will strengthen you when you are tempted. Stay on the path of freedom, my friends.

"Our new believer's class will be held this Wednesday night. This is a chance for those of you who have recently come to Christ to learn more about what it means to follow Jesus. Following Jesus is not merely talking the talk, but it's walking the walk. In fact, the Bible says if we are true believers we must walk as Jesus did.

"For those of you who have taken the 3t Challenge be sure to let me know how it's going. If you're a visitor, the 3t Challenge is our way of giving our time, talents, and treasures to God. If you can't make it back to our service tonight, please email or call me and let me know how you are doing in your spiritual journey. Exciting things are happening around New Hope and Westside with this 3t Challenge."

Pastor Victor then led a powerful prayer for God to move His people in a mighty way.

As Julius prayed, he had no idea the great challenges he was about to face.

Chapter 2

After the service, Victor and Maria Martinez went over to eat at Hector's house. Reginald and Julius joined them. As the ladies prepared the pot roast, the men talked in the living room.

"That was a great sermon this morning, Pastor Vic." said Julius.

Victor replied, "Thank you, Julius. I am really proud of how well you are handling all of the changes you are going through. Are you ready for our next meeting this afternoon?"

"Yes, sir. I'm nervous about it, but I'm ready." answered Julius.

"What are you doing today?" asked Reginald.

Julius answered, "I'm getting close to the end of my list. As you know, Pastor Vic asked me to pray about who the Lord wanted me to make restitution to. There were seven people who I felt like God wanted me to ask forgiveness from. I have gone to five of them and asked for their forgiveness. All five of them not only forgave me, but encouraged me to stay on this path. Today, I am going to meet with Mr. Lang, the high school principal. I did a lot of bad things there. I'm not sure how he's going to respond. Man, I hate doing this, but I know God wants me to own up to what I've done."

Victor said, "You have done a great job of asking forgiveness from those you have wronged. I was proud of you for mowing Ms. Chan's yard the past two weeks. That, combined with paying her back for the lawn mower that you had stolen from her, was good. I'm happy she decided not to press charges."

"Me too!" replied Julius.

Victor added, "Now remember, these good works will not save you. Salvation is found only in God's grace, through faith in His Son Jesus. It is a free gift. When we are saved, we will change. This change is the evidence of our new life in Christ."

Reginald said, "True, Pastor. But I have to say, Julius, it is awesome seeing you owning up to your mistakes. God will bless your obedience."

Julius answered, "He already has! One guy, Malcolm, who I had stolen some money from, freaked out when I brought his money back to him with interest last week. He was still mad at me at first, but when I explained why I was returning it, he was amazed. I got to witness to him and he was at church this morning! He told me he hadn't been to church since he was a little kid."

"Wow! That's awesome." exclaimed Reginald.

Just then police sirens could be heard going by the house.

Victor said, "I hear those sirens a lot more than I would like."

Hector asked, "Did you hear about the two young men who were killed last night? They shot each other downtown in the middle of the night. One died at the scene. The other died on the way to the hospital."

Julius said, "I'm sure drugs were involved. Man, it's rough down there. I hate to hear about these guys killing each other."

Victor thoughtfully added, "What a waste."

Maria called out, "Lunch is ready, guys. Come and get it."

The mood lightened when they sat down to eat. Everyone enjoyed eating lunch together. Maria and Elizabeth were in extremely good moods. They kept looking at each other and giggling like school girls with a secret.

After lunch, Victor and Julius drove over to Principal Lang's home. On the drive over, Victor pointed out to Julius all of the young men who were just hanging out around the city. He explained to Julius how important it was to use his time wisely and not waste it.

Victor had called the principal earlier in the week and set up the meeting. Julius began by sharing his recent Salvation experience with his principal. Then he confessed every sin he could remember committing at Westside High School.

Principal Lang patiently listened to Julius. When he was finished, his principal told him he had his forgiveness, but there would be consequences for his actions.

They worked out a plan for Julius to re-enter school immediately. The semester had just started, so he would be able to catch up quickly. He would have enough credits to graduate on time if he took a full load the next two semesters. He would also have to work at the school after hours as community service. Principal Lang explained he would allow him to serve at the New Hope after-school program a couple of days a week. Julius would also have to write a paper each week for Principal Lang to grade, detailing what he had done that week to become a better man.

As the meeting was coming to an end Julius said, "Principal Lang, thank you for giving me a second chance. I won't let you down. Would it be all right if I asked you a question before we leave?"

Principal Lang answered, "Yes, Julius. You may."

Julius continued, "As I've told you, Jesus really changed me and I'm a new person because of His love for me. I understand I've messed up bad. I want tell everyone about the forgiveness Jesus offers us."

Principal Lang said, "Yes, Julius. You have done a good job of sharing what Jesus has done for you. I feel like there is something specific you're wanting to ask me."

Julius looked into Principal Lang's eyes, "Are you a believer and follower of Jesus?"

Principal Lang looked at Julius, "Yes, I am. Jesus saved me long ago. I attend Westside Baptist Church. I have been a follower of Jesus for over fourty years. My forgiveness of you today is based on the knowledge and example of God forgiving me. Julius, you have made a lot of bad decisions, but I'm glad to see you are making good ones now. I'll see you at school this week, once you're reinstated."

Victor and Julius thanked Principal Lang for meeting with them. They all shook hands and left.

Chapter 3

As they drove home, Victor said, "Julius, you handled yourself very well back there. You owned up to your mistakes and were humble in accepting your punishment."

Julius replied, "I'm just glad Principal Lang accepted my apology. I realize how stupid I was acting now."

Victor said, "I like the plan Principal Lang came up with. You will be able to pursue your diploma, which is very important. Julius, do you realize people who graduate high school make ten thousand dollars more a year on average than those who don't?"

Julius answered, "I had no idea."

Victor continued, "Another thing is, high school dropouts are eight times more likely to end up in prison."

Julius said, "I didn't know that either. I can believe it though. I was headed down that path."

Victor said, "You will be working after school on campus and over at our after-school program at church. Those duties will teach you some good life lessons. And writing a paper each week will help strengthen your writing skills in case you want to continue your education."

Julius replied, "Continue my education? You mean like college or something?"

He answered, "Why not? I looked at your grades and they are surprisingly good. If you do well this year, you could apply to college or a vocational school. Julius, an education can be a ticket out of poverty. Let's concentrate on getting you back into high school first."

Julius smiled, "God is opening some doors I never imagined might be possible. Thank you, Pastor Vic, for believing in me."

He said, "We still have another meeting tomorrow night. After that one, you should be able to concentrate on school."

Julius shared, "Yeah, I'm not too worried about Mr. Alexander. I went joy riding in his car with his son, Durand. He is two years older than me. He's the one who actually took the car. I just rode along. Durand ended up wrecking the car and we split. I guess that was almost three years ago, when I was fourteen. Mr. Alexander was always a nice man. Durand got worse and worse. He ended up in the pen. He got caught with drugs and a gun. I hate that I wasn't making better decisions back then."

They pulled into Victor's driveway at 3:23 and parked.

Victor said, "Julius, you have repented of your sins and been forgiven by God. You're doing all you can to make restitution to your fellow man. I'll see you tonight at church."

Pastor Victor arrived at New Hope with Maria for the gathering that evening. He loved listening to people share how they were giving God their time, talents, and treasures.

Victor began the service, "Welcome to New Hope Church. I'm excited to see all of you here this evening! As you can tell, our morning service has been very full since the great revival we had a few weeks ago. Many of you are new converts to Christianity, and I am very thankful to Jesus for you. I think it is time to make some room for other people to join us. Three weeks from today we will begin a nine o'clock Spanish language service. All of our songs, programs, and messages will be in Spanish at the nine o'clock service. At our ten-thirty service we will speak English. It's so good that God has blessed us to grow in this way. I would love for our worship team to now come up and lead us in praising God tonight."

Dewayne was playing guitar. Theresa was on the keyboard. John and Nancy Hurst led the singing. As they entered into the songs of worship the Holy Spirit fell upon the gathering. People were openly praising God for His goodness and mercy.

A church whose congregation is made up of more than fifty percent excited new Christians can be thrilling!

As the worship set ended, Pastor Victor welcomed testimonies from the congregation on how they were striving to give God the first fruits of their lives.

Several people shared how they were beginning the habit of sacrificing time each day to read God's word. Victor emphasized how important knowing and memorizing scripture was to living an abundant life for Christ.

Others shared how God was calling them to use their talents to serve the church and community. One man was going out to Redemption Park and building friendships with young men who played ball out there. He brought them water bottles and Gatorade. If they asked him why he brought it, he told them that's what Jesus wanted him to do. He shared how he had been able to witness to several young men this way. Victor told him he was proud of him, but to be careful going out to Redemption Park alone.

New Hope was in a poor area, but many people shared how they were giving as much as they could to God and His people. One lady had paid off some bills for her neighbor who had recently lost her job. Another family was inviting their neighbors over to eat a couple of times a week to help them out. Their neighbors were now coming to church with them.

About an hour after the amazing service, most people had headed home. Victor, Hector, Maria, and Elizabeth were talking.

Hector said, "What a great night! Hey, Victor, how did it go with Julius and his principal today?"

Victor replied, "It went great. I think he's in good shape to get back in school and graduate on time."

Elizabeth added, "That's wonderful. I'm glad Principal Lang was understanding about the situation."

Victor said, “He really was. He came up with some good, healthy punishments for Julius too."

Maria said, "I bet he didn't come up with those 'good, healthy punishments' all on his own."

Victor smiled, "He's a very smart man. I'm sure he would have thought of those without my help, if I had let him."

The group laughed.

Maria said, "Well, we better get home. I need to get my rest. And so does Elizabeth."

Then the ladies giggled way too much at that statement. Victor and Hector looked at each other wondering what had gotten into their wives.

Chapter 4

When Victor and Maria got home, Victor asked her, "What's gotten into you and Elizabeth? You two have been acting silly!"

Maria said giggling, "What are you talking about? Okay, I have something for you. Sit down on the couch."

As Maria went back to the bedroom, Victor laid his Bible down on the coffee table and sat down on the couch.

He said, "You are acting very weird, Maria. What are you up to?"

She answered, "You just calm down. I'm almost ready."

Maria walked back into the living room with a wrapped present. "Here you go!"

Victor asked, "A present? It's not my birthday."

Maria replied excitedly, "Open it already!"

Victor tore open the present. He removed the top of the box, "A t-shirt? Why do I need a t-shirt?"

Maria squealed, "Read it, Silly!"

He removed the white t-shirt from the box and held it up, reading aloud, "World's Greatest Dad!"

Maria grinned from ear to ear.

He lowered the shirt and said, "But, Maria, I'm not a...are you telling me that...are you pregnant?!"

She exclaimed, "You're going to be a Papa!"

Victor jumped to his feet and grabbed Maria. Picking her up, he gave her a huge hug. Then he sat her down and started jumping up and down, pumping his fist and yelling, "I'm going to be a Papa!"

After several minutes of rotating between yelling, jumping, and hugging Maria, he settled down a little. He asked all about the details of when she found out and what she had been through.

She explained, "I think I'm about six weeks pregnant. I've been having morning sickness for several weeks. It hasn't been easy hiding it from you."

Victor said, "You're very sneaky. I had no idea. I've noticed you have been going to bed earlier."

She replied, "That's because I have been exhausted. I'll get to sleep and then wake up for no apparent reason. This little baby of yours is already wearing me out!"

He said, "So this is why you and Elizabeth have been acting so silly. We need to call my cousin, Hector, and let him know!"

Maria replied, "We will not be calling them until ten o'clock tonight. Elizabeth has not been acting 'silly' because I am pregnant. You see, Hector is going to be a daddy again! She's about three weeks ahead of me. We agreed to tell both of you tonight and call at ten o'clock."

With a big smile on his face Victor said, "Hector is going to have another little one? He is going to be so happy. God has really blessed our family. Maria, I love you so much."

The couple shared a long, romantic kiss.

Just before ten o'clock the Martinez's doorbell rang. Victor answered it. Hector burst through the door and hugged Victor.

Hector exclaimed, "Hey, Cuz! I hear you're going to be a papa!"

Victor replied, "Yes, I am! And I hear Pedro is going to be a big brother! Congratulations!"

Elizabeth stepped into the house, holding the hand of their two-year-old son, Pedro. Maria walked into the living room.

Elizabeth said, "I know we were supposed to call, but Hector insisted we come over."

Maria answered, "I totally understand. These two are something else. Victor just about hit his head on the ceiling jumping for joy!"

Everyone laughed. Elizabeth laid Pedro down in the guest bedroom.

Hector said, "I think I am having sympathy cravings. Some pickles and ice cream sound good." They all laughed again.

They talked and told stories until almost midnight.

Hector told them how Elizabeth had put a shirt on Pedro that said "#1 Big Brother". He played around the house for a little while. Finally, Elizabeth asked Hector what Pedro's shirt said. Hector, like Victor, didn't catch on immediately. But when he did, raw emotion and joy overflowed from deep inside of him.

They took some time to pray for their families and their tiny, growing babies. Finally, around midnight, the Gonzales' went home.

Victor was so excited, he stayed up most of the night thinking about all of the changes a baby would bring.

Chapter 5

Monday morning, Victor met with an applicant to be his associate pastor. New Hope Church was growing quickly and Victor felt it was time to get some help teaching and discipling people. He definitely wanted someone who spoke English and Spanish fluently. Ramone Johnson, the young man he interviewed, was bilingual and very intelligent. He had recently married Mia, a young lady from Westside.

Ramone had grown up the son of a missionary who served in Guatemala and Mexico. Having gotten his undergraduate degree in History, he was planning on entering law school until God called him to preach. Ramone had attended two semesters of seminary and worked as an intern in a big church in the capital city. He could finish his seminary degree going to the school campus a couple of days a week in the capital city, and take the rest of the courses online.

Victor was reviewing his notes on Ramone when the phone rang.

He answered, "New Hope Church, Victor Martinez speaking. How may I help you?"

An enthusiastic voice on the other end said, "Pastor Victor. This is Gabriel Lopez. How are you doing?"

Victor replied, "Gabriel! I'm great. How are you?"

Gabriel answered, "I am doing good. Actually, I'm doing fantastic. My unit will be returning stateside this weekend. We're one month early. I was wondering if you could do me a favor?"

He answered, "Anything, Gabriel. What can I do?"

Gabriel explained, "I would like to surprise Sofia when I come home. We are scheduled to land Sunday morning at nine a.m. Could you have someone pick me up at the airport in the capital city. They could bring me straight to the church and at the end of the service you could bring me out to see Sofia. She would be really surprised."

Victor agreed, "I love the idea. I will make sure someone will be there to pick you up. Gabriel, I am happy you are coming home to us! May God bless you and your safe return. This is an answer to some passionate prayers."

Gabriel said, "I'm so ready to be home with my family. Thank you and Maria for taking care of them for me. I know Westside can be dangerous, especially for a woman who's alone. It is very hard being away when your baby is born."

Victor replied, "I can't imagine. You are a true hero, Gabriel. I'm very proud of you."

Gabriel said, "Thank you, Pastor. I have to go. See you Sunday."

Victor said, "Goodbye."

Julius met Victor at New Hope at four o'clock on Monday afternoon. Julius was excited and ready to finish his list of asking people for their forgiveness. All of the previous visits had gone well.

Julius entered Victor's office and asked, "Hey, Pastor Vic. How's your Monday treating you?"

Victor replied, "Very well. Thank you for asking. I interviewed a wonderful candidate for the associate pastor position. The kids are having a great time in the after-school program. I couldn't be more excited about finishing this list with you today. Are you ready?"

Julius answered, "I'm more than ready. God has really been blessing me. I had my quiet time this morning and then went by and got everything filled out to get back into high school. I'm going to be the best student Westside has ever seen!"

Victor laughed, "Great, Julius. Let's head over to Mr. Alexander's. I called him and left a message on his phone earlier. Hopefully he'll be home."

Julius replied, "Awesome! Let's roll."

As the men rode over to Mr. Alexander's house they passed two police cars with their lights flashing. The officers were loading three African American young men into the back of their cruisers. Victor said a quick prayer for his community.

Mr. Alexander only lived about two miles from New Hope Church. They arrived and had a short word of prayer for wisdom. Julius knocked on the door.

Mr. Alexander answered it and said, "I got your message. Come on in. Have a seat. I'm not sure what this is about, but it's nice to have some company. What can I do for you gentlemen?"

Julius began, "Mr. Alexander, thank you for allowing us some time to speak with you. I'm not sure if you remember me, I'm Julius Williams. I have recently given my life to Jesus Christ and I am doing my best to follow him. I ran around with your son, Durand, a few years ago. I was fourteen and he was sixteen. One time, when we were hanging out, he decided to take your car and go for a joy ride. I went along with him. Durand wrecked your car that night. I would like to ask for your forgiveness. While it wasn't my idea, I did go along with it and I didn't report the accident. For that, I am truly sorry."

Mr. Alexander was silent. When he finally spoke, he angrily said, "It was boys like you that led my Durand into a life of crime. Do you know where he is today? He's in prison! Because of bad friends like you!"

Julius was shocked. How could Mr. Alexander think a boy two years younger than his son would be the bad influence in this situation?

Julius explained, "Mr. Alexander, I looked up to Durand. I wanted to be like him. I just went along with what he told me to do."

Mr. Alexander asked, "What he told you to do?"

Julius answered, "Yeah. It was his idea."

Mr. Alexander, his voice now filling with rage, "My Durand was a good boy. He got mixed up with the wrong crowd and now he's the one suffering!"

Victor interrupted, "Now let's calm down and think about this. Julius is here today asking for your forgiveness in a situation your son put him in. Durand was probably influenced by other bad friends, but in this case, it was Julius who was pressured into doing something he knew was wrong. He's here owning up to it and admitting it was wrong."

Mr Alexander yelled, "Get out of my house! Both of you! And don't come back. Do you hear me?!"

Victor and Julius stood and walked out the door.

Julius humbly said, "I just wanted to say, I'm sorry."

Mr. Alexander replied, "Get off my property and stay off!"

Victor drove Julius back to New Hope Church. They were very disappointed. Victor explained to Julius how Mr. Alexander wasn't thinking logically, but was being led by his emotions. His son was in a bad place and he was angry about it.

Julius was discouraged.

He asked, "So what am I supposed do now? I asked for his forgiveness and he won't give it."

Victor answered, "The Bible says in Romans 12:17 and 18, 'Never pay back evil for evil to anyone. Respect what is right in the sight of all men. If possible, so far as it depends on you, be at peace with all men.' Julius, you have gone the extra mile to make restitution for your sins. Let's take the next few days and pray about how to handle this. God is in control and He is working. Maybe through this, Mr. Alexander can face some of his emotional issues and find some peace of his own. Obviously, he is a man who is hurting."

Julius said, "I never thought about how much pain he might be going through. I guess when a child makes bad decisions it can hurt their parents as bad as it hurts them."

Victor replied, "That's very insightful, Julius. Go home to your mom and share with her what you learned. I know she'll appreciate it."

"I will, Pastor Vic." Julius answered.

The men went home, not realizing what life changing events they had set in motion.

Chapter 6

Tuesday, Victor went to lunch with Hector and Ramone. He wanted a chance to get to know Ramone outside of the church. He also wanted Hector's opinion of the young man. They were both very impressed with him. He came across as mature, and he had a good sense of humor. They explained the 3t Challenge to Ramone during lunch. He told them how Mia had taken the challenge and also told him about it.

Ramone asked, "Who decides how people are to use their time, talents, and treasures? What if someone disagrees with the way I spend mine?"

Hector answered, "It's up to each individual to decide. They may ask for advice or counsel, but ultimately we are all responsible for our own actions. Of course, Victor is the pastor, so God blames him if someone messes it up!"

The men laughed.

Victor said, "Hector is right about it being each Christian's duty to use their 3t's for God and to follow Him the best they know how. Eternal life is God's gift to us, we can't do anything to earn it. The 3t Challenge is simply our way of organizing our lives to follow Jesus. It doesn't add to our Salvation."

After lunch, Victor was walking back into New Hope when his cell phone rang.

He answered, "Hello."

Maria spoke quickly, "Victor, you have to get down to the police station! Julius was arrested at his house a little while ago!"

Victor asked, "Arrested? What happened?"

Maria answered, "I didn't get any details. You can imagine how upset Wanda Williams was when she called. She was crying uncontrollably. Just get down there, please."

"I'm headed there now. Maria, trigger the prayer chain. We need God's help!" said Victor.

He drove straight to the police station. It took some time to figure out what was going on. In between questioning the front desk about the situation, Victor contacted a lawyer, Kevin Cathey, who was an African American member of New Hope.

As the day wore on, Victor was able to learn more details. It turns out Mr. Alexander had filed a police report on Julius. The police put out a warrant for his arrest, on charges of being an accomplice to grand theft auto. The police served the warrant and arrested Julius at his house. He lost his cool and they added resisting arrest to the charges. Kevin was able to get bail set at five thousand dollars. He would have to pay ten percent of it to be set free. Victor lined up the money as quickly as he could, and Julius was released about eight o'clock.

Julius walked out from behind a locked door into the police station's lobby where Victor was waiting for him.

Julius shouted angrily, "What's going on with this? It's ridiculous! These fools are..."

Victor stepped forward and said in the sternest voice Julius had ever heard, "Shut your mouth and come with me."

Shocked by the pastor's words, Julius obeyed.

As they got into the car, Victor said, "Julius, if you act like a thug they will treat you like one. I understand you're upset. You have a right to be. There is a time and a place to release your frustrations. We're going to the church. You will have time to vent there."

Julius remained quiet for the rest of the ride.

They arrived at the church and went inside. Wanda Williams, Maria, Reginald, Hector, and Kevin Cathey were all there waiting for them. Wanda ran and hugged her son. After the emotional reunion, Victor explained, "This is going to be a long night with a lot of high emotions. Kevin is the professional here. Let's all give him our attention and try not to interrupt while he explains what's going on."

Kevin began, "There has been a lot going on today. Mr. Alexander had an arrest warrant issued this morning for Julius' involvement in the theft of his car just under three years ago. The statute of limitations on this crime is three years, so unfortunately the charges will stand."

Julius exclaimed, "Yeah, but I..."

Victor interrupted him, "Julius! Be quiet and listen. You will have plenty of time to share after Mr. Cathey is finished letting us know where we stand legally on this issue."

Kevin continued, "Thank you. Like I was saying, the charges will hold up. Julius has admitted to many people he committed this crime. I spoke with the prosecutor's office. They agreed since the crime occurred several years ago, they wouldn't pursue maximum charges. However, Julius has a juvenile record of drug use. This takes away the chance of them going for probation only. If this goes to court, Julius will most likely spend the next six months to one-year in the Westside Juvenile Detention Center..."

Wanda Williams broke down sobbing. Maria comforted her and everything stopped until she composed herself.

Kevin began again, "If Julius' sentence goes past his birthday in December, which it probably will, he will be moved to a regular prison for the remainder of his time. I spoke with Pastor Victor about an alternative. There is a place for rehabilitation. It is a Christian-based program called Second Chance Ranch. It's located four hours north of here, outside the city of Kingsland. Julius can finish high school and even get a jump on some college courses there, if he chooses. The prosecutor handling the case said she would agree to the plea bargain, but we have to have an answer by tomorrow morning at nine. My legal advice is to take the deal. If Julius completes this program his record will be wiped clean. The decision is up to you, Julius."

Julius looked up from the table and asked, "Doesn't sound like much of a choice. Will they take me?"

Victor said, "I called in some favors from a friend who knows the camp's director. Space is limited. They have one opening. He said you could have it, if you want it."

Wanda asked, "When could Julius come home? Will he be able to call me?"

Kevin said, "You have to realize this is a facility where kids are being rehabilitated. It's not church camp. They will be tough on Julius, but fair. If he chooses to embrace the situation, he can get a lot out of it."

Julius stated flatly, "I'll take the deal. Set it up."

Kevin replied, "Professionally, I think you're making the right decision. Personally, I hate this for you and your mom. But remember, Julius, God has a plan and always works for His children's good."

Wanda softly said, "Julius, let's go home."

Victor interrupted, "Not yet. Julius and I need to have a talk. Man to man."

Julius looked at Victor incredulously and said, "What is that supposed to mean?"

Victor answered, "Kevin, thank you for your hard work today. We will meet you at the courthouse at eight-thirty tomorrow morning. Wanda, I would like for Maria to take you home. Hector and Reginald, you have work early tomorrow. Go get some rest. Julius and I have some issues to deal with here. Then I will bring Julius home. Is that all right with you, Sister Wanda?"

Wanda replied, "Whatever you feel is in the best interest of Julius. I trust you, Pastor."

The ladies left for Wanda's house. They discussed the situation all the way home. Wanda was upset, but she wasn't angry. She told Maria how Julius had never known his dad. She had gotten word two years ago that he was in prison. He had never been a part of their lives, so she didn't see any reason to tell Julius about it. She always wondered if that was the right decision. Maria comforted her. She understood decisions for parents are very difficult. Being a single mom makes them even tougher. Wanda's sister arrived and after some prayer, Maria went home. She was exhausted.

Back at the church, Victor started in on Julius, "You were all fired up back at the jail. Why are you so quiet now?"

Julius just shrugged his shoulders.

Victor said, "Big bad Julius don't care about nothing now. I saw potential in you. Where did that go?"

Julius continued to stare at the ground, trying to ignore Victor.

He continued, "So you've gone from angry to apathetic, huh? Just take whatever feelings you have and shove them deep down inside. Things didn't work out the way you wanted, so now you just shut down like a little kid."

Julius finally snapped, "What do you want me to say? That I'm mad? Yeah, I'm mad! I sell out for God and He disappears! I go the extra mile, like you told me to do, and now I'm headed off to who-knows-where! I could have gone to prison on my own. I don't understand. Things were going just like..," Julius' tone changed and his voice began quivering, "...like they were supposed to. People were proud of me. My mom was proud of me. My dad probably would have been proud of me, if he knew me."

Victor stepped over and embraced Julius as he began to weep. After a long time Victor spoke.

He said, "Julius, these are all very real, very important questions and feelings. It's all right to ask God hard questions and tell Him you're mad about it. He can handle it! And Julius, everyone is still very proud of you. I know you feel like a failure right now, but that is only a feeling. Julius, mature Christians are not led by feelings, they are led by the Truth. That's why we spend time daily in the Word and seek God. Sometimes God gets us all alone through heartbreak, sickness, death, broken relationships, or even suffering injustice to begin teaching us about Himself. He knows what we need to grow."

Julius asked, "So you think God has me in this situation for a reason?"

Victor answered, "I know God doesn't waste a bad experience. And He will grow you through this, if you let Him. Julius, it sounded like you are scared of not knowing anything about this Second Chance Ranch. It would make sense. Is that true?"

Julius answered, "Yeah, I guess. I don't know anything about this place. I figure it's like a miniature prison."

Victor offered, "Why don't we get you home to your mom and look it up online when we get there?"

Julius replied, "That sounds good, Pastor Vic. Thank you for taking care of me today."

Victor answered, "Julius, that's what families do."

Julius wiped the tears away from his eyes and followed Victor to the door.

Chapter 7

Wednesday morning Victor, Julius, and Wanda met Kevin in front of the courthouse. Kevin reviewed the process and reminded everyone to be quiet and respectful.

As they sat waiting for their case to come up, Victor watched all the people who were waiting to stand before the judge. His heart broke for them. He knew his church must do more to help these people in some way. As he was praying for God to show him what he should do, Julius' case came up.

The judge agreed to allow Julius to serve his sentence at the Second Chance Ranch. He explained Julius would have to leave for the ranch no later than Monday morning. Julius agreed and thanked the judge for allowing him this option. As they were exiting the courtroom, Julius saw Mr. Alexander in the lobby of the building. He walked over to him, away from Victor and Kevin.

He said, "Excuse me, Mr. Alexander. May I have a word with you?"

Mr. Alexander looked angry, "If you must. Go ahead and let me have it."

Victor and Kevin noticed Julius missing and hurried over to him as he said, "Mr. Alexander, I'm sorry Durand made some bad decisions. I apologize for my part in some of them. I'm not mad at you for pressing charges. I forgive you. I know my God works all things for the good of those who are His. I hope someday you will forgive me. More importantly, I hope you accept God's free gift of Salvation, if you haven't already."

Mr. Alexander stood in stunned silence.

Kevin said, "Julius, let's go."

As Kevin and Julius walked away, Victor said, "Mr. Alexander, I know you are hurting because of your son. I don't agree with the way you have treated Julius, but I know that hurt people, hurt people. If I can ever help you in any way please call me. Jesus loves you very much. And so do I, through Him."

Mr. Alexander was surprised. He expected his adversaries to attack him.

He turned and walked toward his truck all alone.

Victor caught up with Julius, "I appreciate your attitude toward Mr. Alexander. It's true what you said: God is always in control."

Julius answered, "I know, Pastor Vic! I've been praying and God has given me peace. He's got this."

Victor smiled and silently praised God.

The rest of the week passed quickly. Victor met with many people who were going to be baptized in this Sunday's service. Julius spent time with his mom and friends while preparing to leave. Sunday morning quickly rolled around. Victor called Hector to finalize the plans for picking up Gabriel from the airport and getting him to the church. As the service began, Victor was very excited about being part of this wonderful assembly of God's people. After an opening word of prayer, He shared the news of the Spanish language service beginning in two weeks. Many of New Hope's members were bilingual. The praise and worship was filled with emotion as people worshiped the Lord in song. They had brought in a huge tub for the baptism and twenty-one people were baptized in the service. When Victor baptized Julius he said a few encouraging words to Julius then asked, "Julius Williams, who is the Lord and Savior of your life?"

Julius answered, "The Lord Jesus Christ."

Victor continued, "Upon your public profession of faith, I baptize you my brother, in the name of the Father, the Son, and the Holy Spirit." Then as he lowered Julius beneath the water he said, "Buried with Him in baptism," then lifting him from the depths he said, "raised to walk in newness of life. Hallelujah!"

Julius came up from the water and let out a boisterous yell! He turned and embraced Victor in a big wet hug. The congregation exploded in cheers. Victor smiled and clenched the young man in a bear hug. They released and Victor whispered to him, "I'm proud of you."

A little while afterward, Victor stood to share his message. He preached from the book of John, chapter eleven, where Jesus wept over the death of his good friend Lazarus. Victor explained how Jesus loved people and enjoyed their companionship. He lived his life on mission, but took time to enjoy his friends. Jesus never sought the approval of people, but he loved them. He knew death was the result of sin. Victor shared how Jesus was able to hate sin but love people. Ultimately, Jesus would sacrifice Himself to conquer people's sin problem.

Victor gave the invitation to come forward to pray. Several people responded to receive Salvation, to pray for forgiveness, and to pray for others who they knew needed Jesus. It was an outcry to God for His mercy. Victor loved being part of this movement of God.

As the alter call came to an end and everyone returned to their seats, Victor proclaimed, "It's great to celebrate with all of you who have followed God's command to be baptized."

Victor saw Hector standing in the back of the church. They made eye contact and Hector gave him the "thumbs up" sign.

Victor smiled and continued, "As many of you who are part of our church family here at New Hope already know, Sofia Lopez has a husband in our military deployed overseas. Gabriel Lopez is scheduled to return home one month from today. He left when Sofia was very early in her pregnancy. Little Santiago is two months old and he's in the nursery this morning. Sofia would you mind coming forward for a special time of prayer for your family this morning?"

Sofia took Maria's hand and they stepped forward together facing Victor. The ladies put one arm around each other and Victor put a hand on each of their shoulders and prayed. "Dear Lord, Thank you for this wonderful family."

As Victor prayed, Hector silently opened the door and let Gabriel sneak in and walk about half way up the aisle.

Victor continued, "You have heard our prayers over the past year. Allow us to always know You hear us and, according to Your will, answer all of our prayers. We give you all the glory. Amen"

Victor looked up at Sofia. Then he raised his gaze beyond her and smiled very big.

Sofia noticed him looking past her toward the back of the church. She turned to see the most amazing sight she had ever witnessed.

Her husband stood there in his military uniform with tears streaming down his face as he held their baby for the very first time.

She gasped and ran to her love.

They embraced and their tears mixed together as they kissed and clung to one another.

The church erupted in cheers.

After a few minutes Victor said, "Welcome home, Gabriel! Take your family home and spend some time with them. We'll catch up with you soon."

The Lopez family left to a roar of clapping and cheering.

Chapter 8

Victor arrived at the Westside bus station Monday morning at 6:23. Kevin Cathey met him there. After talking for a few minutes Kevin said, "I have a question for you, Pastor. When I was fresh out of law school, I worked as a public defender. I can't say I always enjoyed defending every person assigned to me. There were times I knew they were probably guilty and didn't respect them.

"However, I do feel like everyone deserves good representation in a court of law. Dealing with Julius in this matter has stirred something inside of me. I don't believe he would have benefitted from going to prison, and I feel good about helping him navigate the system. I feel like God is leading me to actively pursue cases, to take pro-bono, and help those in need. It will cost me time and money. Do you think this is a good way for me to fulfill the 3t Challenge?"

Victor answered, "Kevin, last week when we were sitting in court, I sensed God wanted to help those people in some way. I think it sounds like a really good idea! You could use your talents to help those who need it."

"It will be a sacrifice, but I feel like it's the path Jesus is leading me to follow," explained Kevin.

Victor said, "I'm glad to hear you are being sensitive to the Lord. I'll be praying for clarity as you develop this ministry. Looks like they're here. We'll talk more about this soon."

The two men greeted Julius and Wanda.

Kevin asked Julius, "Do you have everything?"

Julius answered, "I have my Bible, duffel bag, and favorite sneakers."

Victor smiled and asked, "Can Julius and I have a quick word?"

Wanda answered, "Sure."

Victor and Julius stepped a few feet away.

Victor asked him, "Are you ready for this, Julius?"

He answered, "Yes, sir. I believe God has this. He can use it for my good."

Victor said, "I'm glad to hear it, Julius. Troy Speer, the ranch director will meet you at the bus station. He'll be the bald-headed guy wearing the Second Chance Ranch T-shirt. I spoke with him yesterday. He's a strong Christian man. Do your best to learn all you can from him."

Julius answered, "I will, Pastor Vic."

Victor continued, "Do your very best, and write me whenever you can. Maria and I will take care of your mom, so don't worry about her. Concentrate on becoming the man God wants you to be."

Julius replied, "Thank you so much."

The terminal's loudspeaker announced the bus for Kingsland was now loading.

Wanda stepped over and took Julius by the hand. Victor and Kevin said their goodbyes and watched as he and his mom walked to the loading area. They embraced in a long hug. He kissed her on the cheek and then boarded the bus.

Wanda walked back over to the men. They all watched as the bus pulled away carrying Julius to the next chapter in his life.

Four hours later Julius arrived at the Kingsland bus terminal. He grabbed his duffel bag and got off. It had been a long trip. As he entered the small terminal, he looked around for the person who would take him from here.

He heard a man ask, "Julius Williams?"

Julius turned to his right to see a bald-headed man walking toward him. Julius answered, "Yes, sir. I'm Julius Williams. Are you Troy?"

The man answered, "Yes! Yes, I am. You've been on that bus a long time. Are you hungry?"

Julius replied, "Yes, sir."

Troy laughed, "Ol' Victor was right about you. Good manners. I look forward to getting to know you better. Let's grab a bite before we head to the ranch."

The two men went to a diner across the street from the bus terminal. As they ate, Troy gave Julius a brief history of the Second Chance Ranch. He explained how it was started fifty years ago by Jerry Black, a small church pastor who saw the need to invest in young men who had lost their way. He bought about eighty acres southeast of Kingsland that he developed specifically for the purpose of reforming young men. He built a cabin for them to live in and he taught them how to live off the land. This form of survival and discipline seemed to resonate with the young men. This disciplined lifestyle really helped the boys develop into men.

In the last ten-to-fifteen years the camp had really grown and adapted to the needs of today's kids and families. There were now two cabins where the boys could sleep. Each cabin would house six students and one counselor.

There was a larger main cabin with a kitchen and a small gym. It also had a large room where they could eat, hold services, and have classes or seminars. This main room had a large rock fireplace. Outside there was a basketball court, a volleyball area and a fire pit. The boys had school classes, chapel, job training, and computer labs daily.

There was a girls section developed on the other side of the property about twenty years ago. It mirrored the structure and program of the boys' camp. Like the boys, they had live-in trained counselors and a psychologist who visited weekly.

On another part of the Second Chance Ranch property was a family area with four individual cabins. It was built eight years ago to meet the needs of struggling families. It was normally used as short-term care to house families who had lost loved ones or who were trying to save their marriage. This allowed them a place to come and heal together.

In the center of the property was a large pond where you could swim or fish. There was a pavilion with picnic tables, a small dock, and some canoes by the pond. This beautiful piece of land was dedicated to helping people discover that God genuinely loves them, hasn't given up on them, and is truly a God of second chances.

Pastor Black passed away several years ago, but he left a legacy of healing broken lives. Although his congregation was never very large in number, he impacted God's Kingdom by simply being obedient to the Lord. He knew God could use anyone in any situation to do Kingdom work.

As the two men finished eating, Troy asked, "Well, Julius, are you ready to go see your new home?"

Julius took in a deep breath, exhaled, and answered, "Yes, sir. Let's head out to the ranch."

The guys drove about twenty minutes before turning down a gravel road and coming to a metal gate. Over the gate hung a sign that read, "Second Chance Ranch".

Troy said, "Julius, you're riding shotgun, so go open the gate and after I pull through, close it. Make sure it latches when you close it."

Julius answered, "No problem. But I have to tell you, this is a first. I've never had to open a gate for a car by hand."

Troy smiled and said, "It may be called the Second Chance Ranch, but most guys have a lot of first time experiences here."

Julius opened the gate, and after Troy pulled through, he made sure it latched closed. He hopped back in the vehicle and they drove up the gravel road. It was heavily wooded on both sides of the road. They came to a small metal bridge and crossed it. On the other side of the bridge the land opened up to a big pasture and Julius could see the boys' ranch buildings. They were log cabins with rock chimneys and a porch on each one. Off to the side of these buildings was a barn and some pens with animals in them.

Julius exclaimed, "I thought this was going to be a small prison. It's a farm!"

Troy laughed. He said, "Yeah most guys don't know what to expect. We try to live off the land as much as possible. We have two cows, raise chickens, and have a great garden. We used to have horses, but we sold them recently. We have some friends who bring horses out for you to ride on special weekends."

Julius answered, "Horse riding?! I've never done anything like that before."

Troy said, "I told you, you're going to have a lot of 'firsts' here!"

Chapter 9

Julius followed Troy into the largest cabin on the ranch. There were eleven young men sitting in the main room. They were listening to a guy who was talking at the front of the room. They all turned and sized-up Julius as he followed Troy across the back of the room, down a side hall, and into an office. He told Julius to have a seat.

Troy explained, "Those are the guys you'll be living, working, eating, and sleeping with. The man teaching is TJ. He's the other counselor here. Julius, here's a handbook of what is expected of you. Any fighting, disobedience, theft, or trying to sneak out will result in punishment. You're scheduled to be here until next May. If you are unable to follow the rules you will be sent immediately to the state, who will place you in the appropriate correction facility.

"Julius, I hope you take advantage of having a second chance to get your high school diploma and your life in order. This is a place where you can grow mentally, physically, and spiritually. The guys will test you at first. Don't give in to your old ways. You have a great opportunity here. Don't blow it."

Julius replied, "Thank you, Troy. I want to become the man God created me to be."

Troy smiled, "I believe you do. I'm praying you will."

The rest of the afternoon was spent getting Julius fitted in his new uniforms. The boys had jeans, t-shirts, and work boots to wear while doing their chores. They had khaki pants, button up shirts and loafers to wear during school classes. They were also provided gym shorts and t-shirts. The boys had to do their own laundry and if their uniforms got messed up they had to work extra to replace them.

After receiving his uniforms, Julius got a tour of the ranch. Troy showed him to his cabin while the other guys weren't around. He was given a schedule of the coming week's activities and chores. Troy told him each week would be different and if the weather was bad they would adjust the schedule. Each day he was responsible to be up at six a.m. This week, he had to gather the chickens' eggs and deliver them to the kitchen by six-fifteen. The other cabin had to cook breakfast this week. If you didn't cook, you cleaned. He was then to be ready, in work uniform, to eat at seven. From seven-thirty to eight they would have chapel. Then it was time to work around the ranch. His group would be cutting trees this week, preparing firewood for the coming winter. At eleven-thirty he would have lunch. From twelve until four-thirty he would have classes and computer labs. From four-thirty to five there would be free time, but at five o'clock he was to be in the kitchen to help prepare and serve dinner. This was his cabin's week to cook supper. They ate at five-thirty and then had study hall from six to seven. Each night they would have different entertainment or events. Lights out was at ten. This schedule didn't leave much free time at all.

Julius asked Troy, "What about the weekends?"

He answered, "On Saturday we don't have any classes, but you have to do your chores and we do have study hall and chapel. Usually the guys like to play basketball or do something outside."

Julius said, "Man, I love some hoops. That will be fun."

Troy explained, "Sundays are a little different. We sleep in 'til seven. Then do our chores, eat, and go to church in town. After lunch we usually play games or do something fun."

Julius answered, "Sounds good."

Troy said, "Great! Okay Julius, be dressed and in the kitchen at five to help prepare dinner. We're having spaghetti tonight. Any questions?"

Julius confidently said, "No sir. See you at five."

Troy left the cabin and Julius sat on the side of his bunk bed all alone in this strange place.

A few minutes later his roommates entered the cabin.

They came straight to Julius as he stood up. They stared at each other in tension filled silence.

An African American kid announced, "I'm Jamal. I'm in the bunk above you."

Julius answered, "I'm Julius."

Jamal said, "Julius, huh? Well, Julius, this ain't no summer camp. You do what you're supposed to, when you're supposed to do it, or we'll all be in trouble. And no snoring or I'll pop you upside your head."

Julius stared at Jamal wondering if he was serious.

Then Jamal smiled and said, "I'm just messin' with you, bro."

The other guys busted out laughing. Jamal, obviously the cabin's unofficial leader, introduced the rest of the guys.

"That tall red-headed guy is Drake."

Julius bumped knuckles with him and said, "Hey, Drake."

Jamal said, "In my past life I would have a sweet nickname for him, but they are a major no-no for Brother Troy. He is not a fan of nicknames in any form. Okay, this short punk is Sebastian, like the crab in that Disney flick. Blondie there is Kerry. And the Mexican in the back is Max."

Julius bumped knuckles and acknowledged each guy. He thought it was funny Jamal used nicknames on everyone right after explaining how they weren't allowed.

Julius asked, "So what's it really like around here?"

Kerry thoughtfully said, "Man, it's tough at first. Just do what you're supposed to be doing and you'll figure it out."

Jamal said, "It was tougher on Blondie, because he is top-shelf. He originates from the grand city of Lost Creek."

Kerry looked toward the floor.

Julius asked, "Lost Creek? What happened? How did you end up here?"

Kerry just shook his head and turned and walked away. Julius immediately felt the tension in the room.

Jamal answered sternly, "Bad decisions, bro. Just like you. Come on everybody, let's get over to kitchen duty. See you there, Newbie! Don't be late!"

Julius said, "Okay man." He realized he had crossed the line of asking too much too quickly. These guys were already close and he was an outsider. After they all headed out, he finished getting his area organized.

Julius stepped out of the cabin and headed straight for the kitchen. A tall Italian-looking kid caught up with him.

He called out, "Hey man! Wait up."

Julius stopped to wait for him.

He came up to Julius, "Hey, I'm Sergio. How's it going?"

Julius answered, "It's all right, I guess. Just trying to figure this place out. I'm Julius."

Sergio told him, "It's not too bad after you've been here awhile."

Sergio continued to talk and talk. Julius realized he needed to get to the kitchen, but he didn't want to be rude.

TJ, the other cabin's counselor, walked up and said, "Julius, don't you have somewhere to be?"

Julius said, "Yes, sir! Sergio, it's great to meet you. I have to get to the kitchen. We'll catch up later."

Sergio smiled and said, "No problem!"

Julius rushed to the kitchen in the back of the main large cabin. As he walked in Troy said, "Julius, welcome to the kitchen. What time did your schedule say you were to be here?"

Julius looked at his cabin mates who appeared very upset. He answered, "Five."

Troy replied, "According to my watch the current time is 5:08. Do you think my watch is correct?"

Julius said, "Yes, sir."

Troy said, "Well, I guess you are going to learn a lesson tonight on the importance of being on time."

Dinner was prepared and TJ's cabin entered into the dining area just before five-thirty. They would have to do the dishes this week after dinner since Troy's cabin was cooking.

They got their food, sat down, and waited for the other guys so they could pray before eating. Once everyone was seated Troy stood and said, "Men, let's stand and pray."

All the boys stood.

Troy said, "Gentlemen, I'm sure many of you have met our newest member, Julius Williams. We are glad you are here, Julius. One of the responsibilities you have here at Second Chance Ranch is being on time. Tonight you were late to kitchen duty. After I pray, you and everyone in your cabin will remain standing while you eat supper this evening."

Julius looked at Jamal who was intently staring at him. Then he looked over at Sergio. A huge smile crossed Sergio's face and he winked at Julius.

Julius was immediately filled with anger! Sergio had deliberately made him late by acting like he wanted to be friends. He had intentionally kept talking to get him in trouble. Julius clinched his fist tightly wanting to attack the Italian. But there was nothing he could do. Not here at least.

Julius was mad as he ate standing up in silence.

After supper Jamal and the other cabin members caught up with Julius in the bunkhouse.

Jamal shouted, "Man, what's up with you being late? I told you to get over there on time!"

Julius answered, "Look man, it wasn't my fault. That Italian dude, Sergio, tricked me into being late. I could knock him out!"

Jamal said, "Whatever. You just make sure you get where you're supposed to be. I don't like standing up while I eat!"

Sebastian added, "Yeah, bro. Just take care of yo' business. You look tough enough. Jack up Sergio. He's a punk anyway."

Jamal agreed, "Might not be a bad idea. Let him know you're not taking anything from him."

Max, the Hispanic young man, calmly but clearly said from across the room, "Forgive and you will be forgiven."

Jamal replied, "Whatever Max! We ain't in Chapel."

Julius looked over at Max thinking about what he had said. The other guys kept talking up a fight.

Julius finally said, "Max is right. I have to let this go."

Jamal asked, "What? Hey, you do what you gotta do. Just don't mess up again and involve me. Got it?"

Julius replied, "Yeah, I got it."

Jamal said, "How about we head on over to study hall. Julius, think you can be on time for that?"

Everyone left to go over to the main cabin.

Julius and Max were the only ones left in the cabin.

Julius said, "Thank you."

Max asked, "For what?"

Julius answered, "For sharing that verse."

Max explained, "It's fine. It just came to mind and I thought I should say it."

Julius said, "It helped me remember who I am now. I'm a new creation. But man, sometimes it's tough to change."

Max said, "I know. So you're a real believer? Not just saying it for Troy?"

Julius answered, "Yeah, man. Just got saved a few weeks ago. I've been giving it my all. Totally focused. At least trying to be."

Max said, "That's good. I'm sold out for Jesus. The only thing I won't do is be a missionary. God wouldn't call me to be one anyway. Other than that, I'm all His."

Julius thought that was weird. He remembered Pastor Vic saying how we can't come to God on our own terms. But he let Max's comment go.

He said, "I'm glad you're a believer too. I better get to Study Hall. Jamal might kill me if I'm late again!"

Max laughed. The guys headed over to the main cabin together.

Chapter 10

Tuesday morning Julius was already awake when his alarm clock went off at six a.m. He rolled out of bed and threw his clothes on. Max was assigned to show him how to gather the chicken eggs. Julius wouldn't ever admit it, but he was a little scared to reach under those chickens to get their eggs.

Max said, "Just slide your hand under them. They won't hurt you."

Julius cautiously moved his hand underneath the first chicken. It suddenly pecked at his hand. He jumped up and jerked his hand back! Max busted out laughing. After a few attempts Julius got the eggs. It would take a while for him to get used to this. Max encouraged him, but laughed the whole time. The guys dropped the eggs off in the kitchen and headed back to their cabin to get showered and dressed.

At seven they sat down after prayer and ate a delicious breakfast.

After breakfast, Troy asked Julius if he enjoyed eating sitting down better than standing up. Julius said he did. Troy smiled and told him he had done a good job so far this morning. Troy knew discipline balanced with encouragement was a great motivator for young men.

After breakfast the guys cleaned the dishes and tables and went to chapel. They sang a hymn, prayed, and had a short bible lesson on the fruits of the Spirit. Julius enjoyed learning about them, because he didn't know much about the concept of Christian's bearing fruit.

After chapel Julius and his team rode in the back of a truck out into the woods. They cut trees and limbs and loaded them onto a trailer. The other cabin's team was back at the ranch splitting the wood that had already been delivered. They would need a lot of wood to make it through the winter.

At eleven-thirty, lunch was served. Julius had worked up a big appetite.

The guys ate quickly, then headed back to their cabins to change into their school clothes.

On the way back to the main cabin, Julius ran into Sergio and a couple of guys from the other cabin.

Sergio taunted, "Yo, man, want to stop and chat?" All three guys busted out laughing.

Julius said, "I don't think so."

Sergio called out, "Slow down, Newbie! We just want to talk."

A voice from behind the boys asked, "Sergio. Is 'Newbie' that young man's name?"

Sergio spun around and sheepishly answered, "No, sir. I'm sorry, Troy."

Troy sternly said, "His name is Julius. Let's make sure we use it instead of any nicknames."

Sergio answered, "Yes, sir. Sorry, sir."

Troy said, "Get to class guys."

The boys hustled into the big room in the main cabin.

After several hours of corporate and individual school work the guys were released at four-thirty for free time until five o'clock.

Julius was exhausted, but he still arrived early to prepare supper. He wanted to stay out of trouble. After eating and study time all the guys got together in the main room and played board games. Julius thought this sounded boring, but he was surprised by how much he enjoyed it. The games were very competitive and they all had a good time.

At nine-thirty Julius was finally able to lay down in bed. He opened his Bible and began reading in the book of Philippians. In a matter of minutes he was sound asleep with his Bible lying on his chest.

At six the next morning he awoke to his alarm clock going off. Time to do it all again.

By Saturday, Julius had figured out the routine. He was mentally and physically tired, but he was adjusting to his surroundings. He and Max were becoming friends. Troy had taken him aside a couple of times to encourage him and talk to him about his faith.

This morning the guys ate and then went to chapel. Julius really enjoyed the lesson TJ taught from the book of Job. TJ pointed out that just because bad things happen in life, it doesn't mean God has abandoned us. This really encouraged Julius. After chapel they had some free time before study hall.

After study hall the guys ate lunch and Troy mentioned it was great weather to play some basketball. All the guys got excited about playing. Today, they decided to break up teams according to cabins, instead of choosing each player individually.

Julius was pumped to be able to play basketball again. He laced up his sneakers and warmed up with his team. Since he was the new guy, he didn't get to start. Julius sized up his opponents and his teammates as he watched them sprint up and down the court. Troy was really good. He's what they would call a 'baller' back at Redemption Park. Max was athletic, but not great offensively, since he grew up playing soccer. Sergio was the tallest player on the ranch, and pretty good right around the basket. TJ was thick and muscular. Julius figured he played more football in school than basketball. The other guys had a mixture of skill sets, but all were pretty good players.

Julius and Drake got into the game for Troy and Max. Julius made an immediate impact. He got a rebound and pushed the ball up the court quickly, then he hit Drake with a great pass for an easy lay-up. Julius made some jump shots and shut down his man on defense. He came back out of the game at the next break. When he got back into the game Sergio was guarding him. Julius stepped out to the 3-point line and made a shot with Sergio trying to block it. On defense, Julius was guarding Sergio underneath the basket, where he elbowed Julius in the rib cage and made a lay-up.

The play got more physical from there and the other guys were getting chippy with each other. Sergio caught the ball by the basket. He spun around and went up for a lay-up. Julius exploded into the air and blocked his shot, rejecting it way out of bounds! Everyone went crazy laughing and taunting Sergio. On the pass attempt inbounds, Julius broke in front of Sergio and stole the ball. Julius went hard toward his basket with Sergio right behind him. Julius went up to dunk it. Sergio leaped and swung his arm, catching Julius in the side of the head in mid-air. Julius crashed to the ground. TJ and Troy were both on the sidelines watching the play. Troy threw his arm in front of TJ, who instinctively took a step toward the guys to break up a potential fight.

Jamal yelled "What's up with you, Punk?"

Julius jumped up with blood streaming from his temple down his cheek. His fists were clinched and rage filled his eyes ready to attack. Troy was ready to run over and break them up, when all of a sudden, Julius relaxed his fists and looked over at Troy. The rage disappeared. Julius stepped up to Sergio and said, "The old me would be beating you down right now. But in Christ I am a new creation." He then turned and walked away to his cabin. Everyone was amazed by what they had just witnessed.

Troy watched Julius walk away and said hopefully under his breath to TJ, "This may be the spark we've been praying for."

Chapter 11

Saturday night in Westside, Victor and Maria were grilling out with Hector, Elizabeth, Ramone, and Mia. Gabriel and Sofia showed up a little later. They asked Theresa to come over and watch the kids. The weather was unusually nice for this September evening. The men were outside sipping lemonade while they grilled.

Victor said, "Ramone, I'm happy you have accepted the offer to join our church staff. I'm very excited about the opportunity we have to reach more people in the community with you on board and with our new service starting a week from tomorrow!"

Ramone answered, "I'm excited too. I believe God is up to something in Westside and at New Hope."

Hector said, "Gabriel, I bet you're happy to be back home. You didn't eat this well in Afghanistan, did you?"

Gabriel smiled, "We had some interesting meals. I think I ate as much sand in some places as I did food over there."

They all laughed.

Victor asked, "Are you settling back into a routine?"

Gabriel answered, "To be honest, it's tough. Being away so long in war, you forget what it's like to relax and be a civilian."

Ramone said, "I know it's not war, but when I moved here from Guatemala it was a huge change. There are so many things Americans take for granted."

Gabriel said, "Yes, we do. My heart hurt so badly for some of those people who lived there. But we had to be careful. When we weren't in a battle, we still had to be alert to possible attacks from the very people we were there to protect. It's hard to just come home and let it all go."

Hector said, "Well, bro, you can relax here. The only thing I'm going to attack is the meat Victor is grilling."

They all laughed once again.

Maria and the other ladies paraded outside with all the fixings for the fajitas. They also had salsa, cheese dip, and guacamole. They sat it all out on the picnic tables.

Ramone said, "Mrs. Maria I'm glad you volunteered to sing with the worship team in our Spanish service."

Maria said smiling, "Ramone, you can just call me Maria. I appreciate your manners, but I'm not old enough for you to be calling me 'Mrs.', young man."

Hector joked, "Mrs. Maria, can I have some salsa?"

Elizabeth answered, "Hector, you have two pregnant women here. I have a feeling you may not want to press your luck with the 'Mrs.' comments."

Once again they laughed.

Maria said, "Ramone, I'm definitely not the best singer, but I took the 3t Challenge and I am using my small amount of talent to worship God. Of course, I'm not doing it just because of the 3t Challenge. But that is what God used to make me realize I need to get out of my comfort zone and help with the worship."

Elizabeth said, "I'm proud of you. Oh, I just remembered, I ran into Wanda Williams at the store yesterday. She said she hasn't heard much from Julius. Just he made it to the ranch safely and he was doing fine, but that was several days ago when he first arrived."

Victor said, "I contacted the camp director, Troy Speer, earlier today. He said Julius was adjusting well and should be fine. I called Wanda and told her. He said next week Julius is going to have to learn how to milk a cow for his morning chores. Can you imagine what Julius is thinking?"

Hector joked, "Can you imagine what that poor cow is thinking? A city boy trying to figure out where you squeeze to get milk! That could get ugly!"

Everyone erupted in laughter.

Victor said, "We need to keep him covered in prayer. God is up to something in that young man's life."

Mia shared, "I'm so happy we are going to be a part of New Hope for the next phase of our life. I love how our church prays and cares for each other. I can see a difference over the past summer. God has big plans here."

Victor noticed Sofia was very quiet.

He said, "We're glad you and Ramone are here too. And Gabriel and Sofia are together and whole once again. This meat is ready! Hector would you pray over our meal for us?"

They joined hands and prayed for the meal, for each other, and for Julius.

Chapter 12

Sunday morning at the ranch had a totally different feel to it. The boys slept until seven, did their chores, and then ate breakfast. Then they began to get ready to go into town for morning worship at Kingsland Community Church.

Julius had discovered the girls' camp also attended church there and after the service they would all eat together and hang out as a group for part of the afternoon. The boys loved Sundays.

Once everyone was dressed and ready, they loaded up in the fifteen-passenger van for the drive into town. Julius sat in the front row where he could talk to Troy and TJ.

As they drove Troy told Julius about the history of Kingsland Community Church. It was the church Jerry Black, the founder of Second Chance Ranch, led for many years. At its largest, it had around eighty people. Currently they ran about thirty people, plus the kids from the ranch. It was amazing a church of this size had been able to develop and support a program as impressive as Second Chance Ranch for so many years. Jerry Black had networked a lot of other churches together to support the ranch. TJ mentioned it was sad a lot of the support had stopped. Julius, noticing the tone of the conversation, asked if the ranch was in trouble. Troy cut his eyes at TJ and told Julius the ranch was supported by God's provision. It was up to them to do their work and God to provide the finances.

Julius could tell Troy was overly defensive about the camp's finances. He wondered to himself how much trouble the camp was having.

The boys pulled up to the church. Troy gathered them in a circle by the van and reminded them to be on their best behavior and to use their manners.

The boys entered the church and sat in two rows. An older gentleman in a suit approached Troy and spoke with him. Then he greeted each young man there by name. When he got to Julius he said, "Welcome to Kingsland Community Church. I am Pastor Jay Helm. We are very glad you are here this morning."

Julius shook his hand, "I'm Julius."

Pastor Helm said, "Yes! Julius Williams. I hope your first week at the ranch has been good."

Julius was surprised the pastor knew so much about him.

He answered, "It's been different."

Pastor Helm said, "I'm sure it has. Looks like you took a tumble. I hope you are okay."

Julius reached up and touched the cut on his temple. He answered, "I'll be fine."

Pastor Helm said, "Good! You hang in there and enjoy God today."

Julius answered, "Yes, sir."

He thought to himself, "*Enjoy God? What does that mean? I bet he meant to say obey or serve God today.*" Julius just marked it up to the pastor being old.

As he was thinking, a parade of girls entered the church and sat in two rows across from the boys. This was definitely the girls from the ranch. They were all dressed similarly and had two female counselors with them. Troy and TJ hopped up and went to speak with the female counselors.

A few minutes later the service began. After the welcome and announcements, they had worship in song. A middle-aged man led them in singing from a hymn book. A lady played the piano. Julius was amazed how the same Holy Spirit he had experienced so powerfully at New Hope was in this place. The music style and setting was completely different, but the Spirit of God was undeniable. He also noticed how the camp counselors and most of the church members were raising their hands, kneeling, or outwardly praising God in some way. Pastor Helm rose to preach and shared a powerful sermon. He had a deep voice that seemed to pierce right into your soul when he talked about the grace of God.

Pastor Helm shared, "Jesus said to His disciples in John 14:6: 'I am the way, and the truth, and the life; no one comes to the Father but through me.' It is only through faith in Jesus we can be saved. This faith in God will change everything about us. Paul said in II Corinthians 5:17: 'Therefore if anyone is in Christ he is a new creature; the old things passed away; behold, new things have come.' Don't settle for the pleasures and things of this world! God has so much more for you than you can even imagine. If you have received God's forgiveness, live like a child of the King of Kings. Remember this: A faith that doesn't change you, doesn't save you. There will be evidence of your Salvation in the way you live and the things you do."

Julius was inspired to continue following God's path for his life.

As the guys were leaving, Julius heard Pastor Helm telling each person, "Enjoy God today!"

Julius thought to himself, "*How weird.*"

After the service, the guys and girls all traveled to a local park where there was pizza waiting for them.

After praying for the meal, the boys let the girls go first in line.

Julius and Max were walking toward the picnic tables. A young lady called out to them, "Hey, Max. You and your friend can sit with us."

There were three girls at the table. The guys went over and sat with them. Max said, "This is Heather, Holly, and Katie. Girls, this is Julius."

Heather, the girl who had called them over to their table, said, "It's very nice to meet you, Julius. How has your first week at the ranch been?"

Julius answered, "It's been okay. Max has helped me survive."

Katie said, "Yeah. I heard you and Sergio have been at it."

Holly interrupted, "Katie! You shouldn't mention that!"

Julius wondered how rumors traveled so quickly through the middle of nowhere.

Julius said, "It's fine. No big deal."

Katie observed, "Well that scar looks like it was somewhat of a big deal."

Julius reached up, again, and touched his wound.

Holly exclaimed, "Really, Katie? You just can't control yourself, can you?"

Heather said, "It doesn't look too bad. Scars are kinda cute on boys."

Max said, "Maybe I should go run my face into a tree."

The girls all giggled.

After they had eaten and everyone was cleaning up their trash, Julius noticed every one of the girls had come up and talked to him.

Max said, "New kid syndrome. Just like at school. Everyone is curious about the new guy."

Julius smiled, "I think they're just talking to me to get closer to you."

They both laughed.

Julius noticed Troy was really hanging close to the girls' camp counselor, Rachel. He wondered if there was something going on with them. The other girl's counselor, Amber, called everyone together. They held hands in a big circle and shared prayer requests and praises. The counselors knew this would take a while, because the students would always drag it out so they could hold hands longer. It was a good way to get the students to share some of their needs and pray together though.

After prayer they loaded up and headed back to their respective camps.

That afternoon, after they got back to the ranch, Troy caught up with Julius. He asked him "What did you think of our outing today?"

Julius answered, "I really enjoyed it! I was surprised by how different the worship music was, but how God was still right there with us."

Troy said, "There are a lot of styles of worshiping God in music. The main thing to remember is we worship for God's glory, not for our entertainment."

Julius said, "The pastor, Jay Helm, really brought the Word. I felt like God was really speaking to me through him."

Troy replied, "Yeah, Pastor Helm is a great preacher and Christian example. He used to preach at a much larger church. He could have stayed there, but he says God called him here. He understands obeying God is the most important thing in life."

Julius inquired, "Pastor Helm kept saying the weirdest thing though. What did he mean by 'enjoy God today'?"

Troy smiled, "I thought that sounded weird when I first heard him say it. I asked him about it one day. He explained to me how many Christians have a sense of having to serve God to get His blessings. The Bible doesn't teach God is an uncaring taskmaster who sits around waiting for us to perform and then rewards us if we are good enough. The Bible teaches that God draws us to Himself and desires a relationship with us. As we realize how wonderful He is, we want to serve Him, because we know He is the best thing we can ever have. Not even His blessings are as good as He is. So just like you can enjoy a relationship with a friend, or you can enjoy a relationship with a girl, you can also enjoy a relationship with God. So, enjoy God today."

Julius said, "Wow. That makes sense. I figured with all the rules and schedules around here, you would view God as a disciplinarian."

Troy explained, "God does discipline people. And He is a God of order, not chaos. Rules and discipline are for our good. But the foundation of Christian faith is a love relationship with Jesus. Not rule-following. We follow God's rules because they are for our good. Julius, do you think your mom loves you?"

Julius answered, "I know she does."

Troy asked, "When she makes rules, do you think it is for your good, or because she is mean?"

Julius answered, "She wants me to be safe and stay out of trouble."

Troy said, "Your Father, God, also makes rules to keep you safe and out of trouble. We follow His rules because we know He loves us, not to gain His love. That's why we should enjoy God. Because He is the most enjoyment we can ever have!"

Julius smiled, "Thanks, Troy. I think I'm getting it."

Troy asked, "Julius, I have a question for you. Usually after a guy meets with the girls' camp for the first time, they are more concerned about when they get to see them again. Or they want to know more about a particular girl. You haven't asked about the girls at all. I'm just wondering why."

Julius answered, "There's definitely some pretty girls in their group. But I don't believe God led me out here to get a girlfriend. He wants me to focus on growing into the man I need to become. He'll provide a wife for me someday when I'm ready."

Troy replied, "Man, I like your mindset. Very few guys understand God cares about all the areas of their life. Even their dating lives. Keep trusting the Lord in all the areas of your life and you won't regret it. Now let's get to supper. I don't want you to have to eat standing up tonight!"

They laughed and headed back to the cabin.

Chapter 13

Sunday morning at New Hope went great. They promoted the two services which were to begin the next week. Ramone was announced as the new associate pastor and he shared his testimony. You could actually feel the excitement of the people realizing something special was happening in the life of New Hope Church.

Victor preached on the Church being the body of Christ. He taught from I Corinthians 12 where Paul says the body is made up of different parts for different tasks. Victor explained how everyone has a different and unique S.H.A.P.E.

He said the "S" is for Spiritual gifts God gives us when we are saved. We are given these gifts to use for building up the Kingdom of God. Not putting them into use is wasteful and wrong.

Victor moved on to "H". He explained it stands for our Heart and is where we see God's love needed. People are sensitive to different needs in the world. Some are drawn to helping the homeless in their community. Others want to help starving kids on the other side of the world. Still others have a passion to help kids learn to read and learn in after-school programs. And the list goes on and on. He taught how God uses our heart to help us choose where to serve.

He taught the "A" was for the Abilities the Lord has gifted us with. Apart from, or sometimes along with, our Spiritual gifts, we have abilities God has given us. As we look at our abilities we can find ways to serve God and help other people. Victor shared how at Big Oak Christian Church, their sister church in Lost Creek, a man who was a mechanic began a ministry to service cars for the needy on weekends. He even took donated cars and repaired them to give to away. One of the members at New Hope had received a car from that ministry. It was such a blessing to a family who was in desperate need of a vehicle!

Victor moved on to the letter "P" which stands for our Personality. He shared how everyone's personality is different. We are made by God, and He can use us for Kingdom work whether we are an introvert, extrovert, or anywhere in between.

Victor continued to the "E" in S.H.A.P.E. He said it stands for our Experiences. Victor was very sober as he explained God knows what we have been through. He shared how God never wastes a bad experience in the life of a believer. We don't always understand why bad things happen to people, but the Lord always works for the ultimate good of those who follow Him.

Victor closed by saying how every member of New Hope has a place they should be serving. He shared how the 3t Challenge allows people to use their S.H.A.P.E. by giving God the first fruits of their time, talents, and treasures. Then he explained how the first steps are to acknowledge Jesus as your Lord, be baptized, and follow Him. In both services the alters were full of people crying out to God.

After the service Gabriel came up to Victor. He asked if they could meet the next day. Victor told him to come by the church around ten o'clock. He could sense something was wrong.

The next morning at eight a.m. Victor got a call from, Leroy White, the mayor of Westside. He asked if Victor could come by his office. Victor agreed to meet him at city hall at one o'clock. He asked the mayor what it was concerning, but the mayor was very vague about what it was he wanted to discuss with Victor.

After several other phone calls and writing some personal notes to church visitors, his ten o'clock meeting with Gabriel came quickly.

Gabriel stepped into the church and called out, "Pastor, are you here?"

Victor laid down his pen and stepped out of his office.

He greeted his friend warmly, "Hey, Gabriel! Great to see you brother. Come on into my office."

The two men shook hands and went back to Victor's office.

Victor began, "It's so great to have you home. I know Sofia is a very happy girl. She missed you tremendously while you were away."

Gabriel replied, "Yes. I missed her also. I'm a very blessed man. Which is why I am so confused as to why I am feeling the way that I am."

Victor said, "Something is obviously troubling you. What's wrong?"

Gabriel paused for a moment, attempting to gather his thoughts. He answered, "I honestly don't know. I looked forward so much to coming back to my family. I'm happy to be home. But it's like I can't adjust to being here. I knew my role and my duty every minute in my company. I took care of my job and my buddies. Now, it's like I'm supposed to just go back to work at the plant, be a husband and get back into my place in this world. But I've changed. I just can't turn it off. Over there we could get blown up just driving to a supply drop-off. Now I drive to work and I worry about an IED being in a fast-food sack in the road. I get to work and there's no feeling of brotherhood. It's crazy, I know. But I can't control it. I think I'm scaring Sofia. I just don't know how to act."

Victor said, "Gabriel, you have been in battle. War changes a man. It is important for you to process these feelings. You're not crazy. You just need some time and help adjusting to life now. I love you Gabriel, but I know you need more help than I can provide. This is an area I can't help you with alone. Will you allow me to make some phone calls and see if I can get someone to counsel you who is experienced in this area?"

Gabriel answered, "Yes. I want to figure this out for the sake of my family. I love Sofia so much. She deserves a husband who can be there for her."

Victor said, "Gabriel, you are there for her. She is a wonderful wife who will be very supportive of anything you need. This isn't something to be ashamed of. I have spoken with people who have needed help and were too prideful to receive it. They almost always regretted not accepting it later. It's wise to ask for and accept help."

Gabriel nodded his head.

Victor got up and moved over to him. He kneeled down, placed his hands on Gabriel, and began to pray. A few minutes later, both men were weeping and calling out to God for wisdom and healing.

After Gabriel left, Victor immediately began checking to see where he could get him some help. He got a call from Maria who told him she had made a four o'clock appointment to see the doctor. She was really exhausted and still having severe morning sickness. She wanted to make sure everything was okay with the baby. He immediately prayed for her and their baby. Then he told her about the call from the mayor. She said she would be praying for him. He ate a quick lunch and headed to City Hall. He wondered what could be so important to have the mayor calling him. They weren't very close, but had met a couple of times at community events. Victor went up a flight of stairs, turned right, and went down a hallway. He approached the mayor's secretary's desk.

She looked up and asked in a very friendly voice, "May I help you?"

Victor introduced himself, "I'm Victor Martinez. I have an appointment with Mayor White."

She replied, "Yes. Pastor Martinez. The mayor is expecting you! Have a seat and I will let him know you are here."

Victor said, "Thank you."

About thirty seconds later the mayor came out of his office and loudly exclaimed, "Victor! I'm so glad you could come by today! Come right in. It has been too long."

Victor was surprised by how the mayor was acting. It was as if they were long lost friends.

As the mayor sat down behind his large mahogany desk, Victor sat down in a leather chair in front of it.

Mayor White said, "Victor, I'll get right to the point. I have had three different people tell me what a great job you are doing at New Hope Church. One told me about your after-school program. Another filled me in on that revival a few weeks ago. And Principal Lang shared with me this past Sunday how you were helping a young man straighten up his life. I must tell you, I am truly impressed."

Victor said, "Thank you very much, Mayor White. God is doing some great things all around me right now."

Mayor White said, "And humble! I love it!"

Victor replied, "I appreciate your accolades, mayor. But I doubt you asked to meet with me in person to talk about what our church is doing."

Mayor White answered, "You are a wise man, just like Principal Lang said. Victor, I would like to make you a job offer. It will be as my Chief of Staff. You will be my advisor on community development and relations. You'll also be my spokesperson for events. Now I realize you are a pastor, but I believe that makes you even more valuable, because of your integrity. And several ministers have felt called to serve a larger community by moving into public service. I know your initial reaction is probably to decline my offer, but I would like for you at least pray over it and give it until the end of the week. Here's a packet explaining the job responsibilities, salary, and benefits package."

Victor answered, "I'm very honored. You are right in saying my first thought is to say 'no.' Out of respect, I will pray over it. May I ask you why you are considering me for this position?"

Mayor White answered, "Victor, you grew up in this community and you are doing your best to contribute to making it a better place to live. You are articulate and can relate to almost everyone who lives here. You would be a great asset to my team. And you would have a lot more say in ways to help our city."

Victor hadn't really thought of it in those terms. He could actually have a voice in ways to help people.

He thanked the mayor for his time and left. When he got to his car, he opened the packet. He was amazed at the salary offer. It was twice as much as he earned at the church. It also offered health care, retirement matching, and a car.

After looking through some more of the paperwork, he put his key in the ignition and turned it. Nothing happened.

Chapter 14

Victor was able to get someone to jump his car and get it started. He bought a new battery and the problem was solved.

As he drove to the doctor's office he was thinking about how nice a new car would be. A larger salary would allow him to provide more for his family. He could still serve the people and God in his new position. Maybe even be able to do more for them.

Victor knew people who had moved out of the pulpit into the business world and been very successful. There were famous politicians who had formerly been pastors. Maybe God was opening this door for him.

He saw Maria as he walked into Dr. Robert's waiting room. Victor said, "Hey sweetheart. How are you feeling?"

Maria stood up and hugged him. She said, "I'm just exhausted and still very sick most mornings."

As they sat down Victor said, "It's going to be ok. Have you already checked in?"

She said, "Yes. We should be going back pretty soon. How did your meeting with the mayor go?"

Victor answered, "It was very interesting. I'll tell you all about it tonight. It's too much to get into right now."

Maria laid her head on Victor's shoulder. A few minutes later they went back to an exam room. Dr. Roberts said Maria's symptoms were normal for a first time mom, but he wanted to do an ultrasound to be sure nothing was wrong. They went down to the ultrasound room and Maria laid on a bed in a dark room. The ultrasound tech was very nice. She made Maria feel very comfortable as she applied some warm gel and rubbed a probe all around her abdomen in several different directions.

Victor asked, "When can we find out the gender?"

The tech answered, "Usually after week eighteen we can check the baby's gender. The further along a mother is the more accurate the results will be."

Victor asked, "Does everything look all right?"

The tech answered, "I'll have to go over everything with Dr. Roberts. He'll share the results with you. But I can show you your baby. Look right here." She pointed to the screen.

Both parents teared up as they looked at the grainy black and white image of their tiny little baby.

After the exam they were escorted back to their original room to await the test results. Maria laid down and Victor pulled up a chair beside the bed and held her hand. A few minutes later there was a knock at the door and Dr. Roberts entered. He said, "Sorry to keep you waiting."

Victor replied, "That's okay, Dr. Roberts. How did the exam turn out?"

Dr. Roberts answered, "Everything looks great! The baby is a little small, but everything looks normal. I'll get you some meds to help with the morning sickness. Maria, you rest as much as needed. These are just side effects of being pregnant."

Maria said lightly, "Praise the Lord."

Victor added, "Thank you, Dr. Roberts."

He replied, "No problem. You take care of yourselves and I'll see you at your next check-up."

When they got home, Victor cooked while Maria rested. Just as he was finishing dinner the oven went out. He was very frustrated as he served dinner.

After eating, Maria asked Victor about his meeting with the mayor again.

Victor said, "It was pretty amazing. The mayor offered me a job. Chief of Staff! Here's the packet with the job description and benefits."

He handed the material to Maria, who sat silently listening. She flipped the packet open.

She said, "Victor! Did you see the salary?"

Victor replied, "Isn't it amazing! It would be such a blessing. And I would get a car."

Maria asked, "But what about the church? We are being blessed so abundantly right now."

Victor replied, "I know. I have to be honest, when my car wouldn't start today, I felt like walking back into city hall and taking the job right then. It's hard to imagine not being a pastor, but we would be so much better off financially. I could help lots of people in this capacity."

Maria said, "We really need to pray. We have some big decisions to make."

Victor replied flatly, "Yes we do. And we have an oven to fix."

Chapter 15

On this Thursday morning, Victor was reflecting on the past week's events. The medicine Dr. Roberts had prescribed helped Maria's morning sickness, which also helped increase her energy level. She was feeling much better. A member of New Hope was able to fix Victor's oven quickly and for free. The after-school program had gained more and more volunteers. On Wednesday night Victor had sat in with the youth. He was amazed by the creative ways they were finding to serve Jesus. Their testimonies were powerful and inspiring. God was definitely moving in many young people's lives. Reginald had shared with him about the increase in the success rate of his ministry. Many of his people were not only staying sober, but were reaching out and helping others who were struggling with addictions.

Victor was very happy to hear these stories. He and Maria were still praying over the decision about his career. As noon approached, Victor prepared to head to a quiet place to pray. Today he was fasting, spending his lunch hour in prayer. He was wondering if his broken car and oven were signs from God that he should pursue the great job opportunity the mayor had offered him. God had not given him any peace about changing jobs or about leaving his church. Victor found himself thinking more and more about what a difference the extra money and the many benefits working for the mayor could mean to his growing family. After praying for clear direction, he went back to his office and checked his emails. He had several messages.

"Pastor Victor, I'm so excited to be a part of New Hope Church! Since I've started coming to church my spirit has been excited. I wake up in the morning ready for another day! I love worshiping God now. You asked to hear how we're doing the 3t Challenge. I'm volunteering in the children's church program. I love those kids!"

-Marilyn Brown

"Hey! You asked for updates on how we're applying the 3t Challenge. I'm ushering in church now. I really enjoy helping people feel welcome. Thanks for sharing with me how I don't have to only sing or preach to have a place in ministry! "

-Theodore Holt

"Pastor Vic! I love my church! As you know I've worked with the after-school program for years. I love teaching those kids how to jam on the guitar! Using my time and talents for Jesus is fun!" – Dwayne

"Hey Pastor Victor, I just wanted to brag on Brother Reginald. Because of God working through him, I am 27 days sober! I know that doesn't sound like much, but to me it's huge! I'm happy to have a church who loves me, just for being me!"

-Sandra Fleming

"Pastor, after taking the 3t Challenge I've joined our neighborhood watch. I'm proud to be a Christian man who is helping protect our community. Sometimes people think of Christians as weak. I'm proud to represent Jesus and do it while I protect my family and neighbors!

-Rodney Beard

"Hey Pastor! For the 3t Challenge I've decided to sponsor two kids from Compassion International. I loved when you shared how we can adopt a child from different countries and know our money goes to help them."

-Casey Fitch

"Pastor, when we first talked about the 3t Challenge at lunch I really didn't think it would make a difference. I was already following God. It's amazing how sitting down and praying specifically about how God wants me to use my time, talents & treasure for Him can make a difference. I love being on your staff here at New Hope and my walk with Jesus is growing everyday!"

-Ramone Johnson

"Victor, this is Pastor Patrick Spakes. As you know I'm on sabbatical. Thank you for the kind notes and messages. I appreciate your prayers and

God is healing my heart from the loss of my son. The reason for this message isn't about any of that. Last night we were going through some letters and notes in Daniel's Bible. I ran across a highlighted scripture and felt overwhelmingly led by the Holy Spirit to share it with you. I sense you are struggling somehow in your spirit. Call me if you need to talk. I hope this helps you in some way.

'But you, be sober in all things, endure hardship, do the work of an evangelist, fulfil your ministry.' 2 Timothy 4:5

Victor stared in stunned silence at his computer screen. God had clearly given him His direction and answered his prayers.

Chapter 16

Two months later, Victor was heading home from a meeting with Mayor Leroy White on a beautiful Tuesday afternoon in November. It was two days before Thanksgiving. Victor had declined the mayor's offer to become his Chief of Staff. Mayor White told Victor he respected his decision, but wished he would reconsider. Victor said he was called by God to be a pastor and he must fulfill his calling.

Since then, Mayor White and Victor had met several times to consider ways to meet the community's needs more efficiently. They were getting the most out of their volunteers and Westside was seeing the difference. Many areas had been cleaned up and looked like new. The homeless shelter was getting more volunteers and much needed additional space. Redemption Park had a new playground for the kids. The police were providing more security for the public's safety. Mayor White and Victor had spent today with other church leaders planning a big community Thanksgiving dinner. New Hope and other area churches would provide and serve the dinner at the city's community center.

New Hope Church had continued to be blessed. The two services were filled each week and a third service was being considered. Their ministries were helping more people than Victor ever imagined they could. The 3t Challenge had helped this surge of volunteerism in the church and community. Several other churches in Westside had accepted the challenge and were actively searching for ways to sacrifice their time, talents, and treasures for God. Victor always stressed Salvation is not by these works, but by God's grace through faith in Jesus alone.

Victor was able to get Gabriel some professional help at the VA hospital in the capital city. He was responding really well to the group therapy. He and Sofia were doing much better. One amazing revelation came from the church's prayer and support of Gabriel during this time. Brother Reginald shared how his brother-in-law had returned home from Vietnam with PTSD. He didn't get any help and turned to substances that led to abuse. His wife, Reginald's sister, got caught up in it as well. Reginald tried to help, but wasn't able to. One night they were both killed after taking a bad batch of drugs. This was one of many reasons, along with the death of his wife, Reginald was so passionate about helping addicts fight for their freedom from substance abuse.

Maria was struggling again with morning sickness. The medicine Dr. Roberts had given her helped for a few weeks, but then it seemed to lose its effectiveness. Elizabeth's pregnancy, on the other hand, was going very smooth. They were all praying for Maria regularly.

Victor's phone rang. He answered it on his hands free device, "Hello."

Maria weakly said, "Victor, please meet me at the hospital. I feel terrible. Dr. Roberts wants me to come right in for some tests."

Victor replied, "No, you stay where you are. I'll be there to pick you up."

Maria said, "Thank you."

Victor rushed to pick up Maria and got her to the hospital as quickly as possible. They arrived and went straight back to the women's clinic where Dr. Roberts was waiting for them.

He said, "Maria, you look so weak. Nurse, get her vitals. Victor, we're going to do our best to figure out what's going on. I'm sorry this has been such a tough pregnancy."

After Maria's vitals were taken, Dr. Roberts ordered IV fluids for her. She was dehydrated. He spoke with Victor while they were getting the IV started.

He said, "Victor, Maria is obviously struggling with this pregnancy and I'm not sure why. We are going to run several tests today. One of them is a something called an AFP screening test. It stands for Alpha-Fetoprotein screening. It's sometimes referred to as the triple marker screening. It tests for birth defects."

Victor asked, "Birth defects? Is this another ultrasound test or something else?"

Dr. Roberts answered, "It's actually a blood test. We'll get a sample of blood and it will give us more information on how we might help Maria."

Victor asked, "So you think there might be something wrong with our baby?"

Dr. Roberts said, "Don't jump to any conclusions. This is a normal test we run. I'm just a little more worried about Maria. We'll keep her here awhile and get her hydrated while we're waiting for the results of the test."

Victor said, "Thank you Dr. Roberts. I'm worried about her too."

After Dr. Roberts left, Victor picked up his cell phone. He called Hector and told him to activate the prayer chain at the church.

A couple of hours later Dr. Roberts came into Victor and Maria's room. He looked very serious as he said, "Maria, we have your test results back.

They all look good except for the AFP test. On this particular test you want to have a low number. We adjusted everything according to your ethnicity, age, and estimated age of your unborn child. The number on the test we got for you is very high."

Victor asked, "What does a high number mean?"

Dr. Roberts answered, "It could mean a number of things, Victor. I'll be completely honest with you. It could possibly mean your baby has spina bifida, where the bones around the baby's spine aren't completely formed. It could mean your baby might have Down Syndrome. Or it could have some other type of chromosomal defect. Unfortunately, the number we're looking at is very high, so it doesn't look good. We'll definitely need to do more tests. I am so sorry."

Victor said, "It's all right Dr. Roberts. Regardless of what we're facing we know God is in control. We love our baby and always will no matter what."

Maria began crying after Dr. Roberts left. She and Victor felt numb, like they were in a bad dream. Victor called Pastor Patrick Spakes to share the news and have Big Oak Christian Church pray for Maria. In a very short time hundreds of people were praying for her and their child.

The next morning was very frustrating. Victor was told the only ultrasound machine in the hospital was down for repairs. A new part was on the way, but it wouldn't arrive before one o'clock. Victor had been up all night praying. Maria was feeling much better, but was very anxious to get the test done. At one-thirty they moved her down to the ultrasound department. The part had arrived and the machine was up and running. They rolled Maria into a dark room. Victor was there with her. She thought about her previous ultrasound. How they had gotten good news and saw their baby for the first time. She was praying God would do a miracle once again. The ultrasound tech was very sweet as she raised Maria's gown and began rubbing warm gel on her stomach. Dr. Roberts entered the room.

He said, "Maria, this test should give us some answers to what we're dealing with today."

She answered, "Thank you."

Victor said, "Many people are praying. We know God can be trusted. Even in the midst of the storm."

Dr. Roberts said, "Your faith in Jesus is amazing. I see so many people who are so hopeless."

Maria said, "Our hope isn't in this world. We live in a world broken because of sin. Death and disease are a part of this life. While our child might have a disease, we will love our baby regardless."

The ultrasound tech began rubbing the wand around Maria's belly.

She paused and gasped. Then she looked wide-eyed over at Dr. Roberts. He was fixated on the screen. He pointed to it and said, "Move back over to the right. Okay, move a little up and laterally."

Victor and Maria were staring curiously at the doctor and technologist who were both grinning from ear to ear now.

Dr. Roberts then exclaimed, "Maria. Victor. Your baby is fine! In fact, both of your babies are fine! Congratulations! You're having twins!"

Chapter 17

Dr. Roberts explained how the AFP test number would also be high in case of twins. Because they missed the second child when Maria had the earlier ultrasound, he didn't consider twins being a possibility.

Victor and Maria cried and celebrated together. They called family and friends to share the good news. Everything looked great with both the babies. Severe morning sickness is common in some women with twins. Knowing this gave Maria extreme peace. Dr. Roberts wanted to keep her overnight to make sure she stayed hydrated.

They had several visitors throughout the afternoon and early evening. Victor asked to stop visitation at seven, so Maria could get some good rest. He walked Brother Reginald and some other church members out to the front lobby. On his way back to Maria's room he walked by a hospital room with the door open. As he passed by the room he glanced in and recognized the patient. It was Mr. Alexander. Victor paused for a moment then took a step back toward the open door. He lightly knocked on it and said, "Mr. Alexander. May I come in?"

He was laying there with oxygen tubing wrapped over his ears going down into his nose. He had monitors attached to him and a faint beeping noise could be heard. He replied, "I wasn't expecting any visitors. I guess it will be fine."

Victor stepped into the room beside the bed and said, "I was just passing by your room and saw you. Maria is here in the hospital too. How are you feeling?"

He gruffly replied, "If I felt good I wouldn't be in here. I'll be fine. Just getting old. The doctor said something about a heart cath tomorrow. I'm not sure exactly what that means. Looking for some sort of blockage. I don't understand most of what they say anyway."

Victor said, "They have some very good doctors here. I'm sure they will take good care of you."

He replied, "We'll see. I've always taken care of myself. I don't like having to trust other people to do anything for me."

Victor said, "An independent spirit. That can be a good thing. Ultimately, though, we really do need each other and God."

Mr Alexander said, "God? You sound just like that Julius kid. All he talks about is God and what God is doing all around him."

Victor questioned him, "Julius? You've spoken with Julius?"

He answered, "No, I haven't spoken with him. I get a hand-written letter from him every Tuesday though. He tells me all about how God is growing him into a good man. He tells me how he's forgiven me and how he's praying for me and my son, Durand. It's ridiculous! He's supposed to be locked up being punished."

Victor said, "So he writes you every week. What else has he said?"

He replied, "He has a friend named Max, who's praying with him for the whole camp to be saved. So far a kid named Jamal and another named Drake have become believers in Jesus. There's another kid named Sergio who's always giving Julius a hard time. He also bullies some of the other kids too. The camp director, Troy, is a great guy who is helping Julius a lot. The other counselor, TJ, is also a big time Christian."

Victor knew all this already because Julius emailed him weekly. He was amazed at how interested Mr. Alexander sounded about Julius and what he was going through. Mr. Alexander sounded like he was talking about a friend. He really didn't have any family or friends that Victor knew of. Maybe God was using this situation to reach him.

Victor said, "Wow. That's something else. Wonder why Julius tells you all this?"

Mr. Alexander replied, "I have no earthly idea. Crazy kid gets thrown in prison and bothers me all the time with his stories."

Victor could sense through his complaining he was secretly enjoying someone including him in their life. Someone was thinking enough about him to take the time to write him a letter every week. Victor had an idea.

He asked, "Mr. Alexander, did you get your letter from Julius yesterday?"

Mr. Alexander gruffly answered, "I have no idea. I came to the hospital two days ago. Why would I care anyway?"

Victor replied, "I could go get your mail for you, if you would like."

Mr. Alexander, a little more softly, replied, "Well, there may be a bill or two I need to look at in there. It will be fine if you don't mind going by and getting it. And if there's a letter from that boy, I guess you could bring it up here too."

Victor smiled and said, "Okay. No problem. Would it be okay if I prayed for you?"

He said, "I guess if you want to you can."

Victor prayed verbally for Mr. Alexander's physical healing and silently for his spiritual healing.

The next morning was Thanksgiving. Victor had Mr. Alexander's mail. In it was a letter from "Mr. Julius Williams." Victor was proud of Julius. He hadn't even shared how he was reaching out to Mr. Alexander.

When Victor went by Mr. Alexander's room he wasn't there. Victor left his mail on his bedside table. On his way out he stopped by the nurses' station. She said Mr. Alexander was having a procedure. Victor prayed for him as he walked back up to Maria's hospital room. He and Maria watched the Thanksgiving Day parade together on TV and prepared to be released to go home.

About eleven o'clock Victor ran back by Mr. Alexander's room. He got permission and went in to visit him. Victor noticed the letter from Julius was opened.

Victor asked, "How are you feeling?"

He replied, "Not feeling much right now. The anesthesia hasn't completely worn off. I'm glad God made drugs for this."

This was the first time Victor had heard Mr. Alexander acknowledge the possibility of there being a God.

Victor said, "Yes, it is. God makes things for a purpose. Drugs are great if they're used for the right reason. If they're not they are ugly and awful."

He replied, "You got that right. They put a stent in my heart. They said it should let more blood flow. I should be fine."

Victor said, "The nurse told me everything went great! I'm very glad it went well. Hopefully you'll recover quickly. I've asked our church to be praying for you. Did you read your letter from Julius?"

Mr Alexander said, "I opened it, but I couldn't see it good enough to read it."

Victor said, "Would you like me to read it to you?"

He replied, "Sure. Make yourself useful."

Victor realized Mr. Alexander wanted people to care about him, but kept his guard up so he wouldn't get hurt. His grouchy demeanor was his way of protecting himself from more disappointment.

Victor pulled the letter from the already-opened envelope and read,

"Mr. Alexander, Hey it's me, Julius, again! I'm not sure if you're getting these letters or reading them, but I hope you are. The Second Chance Ranch has been such a great

place for me to grow and mature. God has blessed this ministry and I'm so glad I'm here. I got to share my Salvation testimony last week at the church we attend in Kingsland. It was great reminiscing about the night God saved me. I didn't even know the revival was going on with Pastor Patrick preaching. God just led me to it. And to Him in the process!

Pastor Helm at Kingsland is a great guy too. He still tells us all the time to 'enjoy God.' (I explained what that meant in a previous letter.) Isn't that cool? And I am learning to enjoy God. Troy is teaching us awesome stuff around here all the time. I'm on track to finish high school in late May. I've also had the opportunity to sign up for some online college credits. If everything goes good, I'll have nine credits to apply to a college, if I go. Can you believe that?"

Victor glanced over at Mr Alexander who had his eyes closed, but was smiling a thin grin.

Victor continued, *"Troy told me the other day that I might be able to come home for Christmas! They reward students, who have stayed out of trouble, with a couple of days home for the holidays. I'd love to be there for my birthday and get to see my mom. I'm pretty sure I'll be able to unless something crazy happens. I can't wait!*

I'm picking up some vibes the ranch might be struggling with funds. Troy always says God will take care of the money. While I believe him, I wonder what's going on. There were some guys in suits here the other day. I think they were from a bank. Troy seemed a little bit stressed after their meeting. I'm praying God takes care of whatever is going on. This is such a great place for people who need it.

I'm glad God used you to get me here. I know it wasn't your intention to help me, but God knew what He was doing. If you ever want to write me back you can. I'm praying for you!

God Bless you and Durand,
Julius."

Mr. Alexander said, "That boy is a mess."

Victor replied, "It sounds like there's a lot going on up there."

He said, "Yes, it does. Not that I care anything about it, but thank you for reading it to me."

Victor could sense Mr. Alexander softening toward him a bit.

Victor said, "I didn't mind at all. I'll let you rest now. The nurse said if you feel up to it they will discharge you in the morning."

He said, "Yeah, I guess they will. I'll probably just take a taxi home."

Victor replied, "I don't like the thought of you going home alone. We're having a quiet, day-after Thanksgiving lunch at our house tomorrow. I could come pick you up from the hospital and we could eat together. I can take you home afterward. It's no problem, since Maria will be resting. If I have to take care of her anyway I might as well take care of both of you for the day. What do you think?"

After sitting quiet for a minute Mr. Alexander asked, "Are you making giblet gravy to go with the turkey?"

Victor smiled, "Of course!"

Mr. Alexander said, “Deal!”

The two men laughed. God was doing something here.

Chapter 18

About a month later, Julius was in the gym working out with Max. Both young men were in great shape and very athletic. They were doing full-body circuit training today. After their workout, Max headed back to the cabin to shower and change. Julius stayed to do a few extra sets of abs. The next day was Christmas Eve and he was ready to see his mom and friends. Troy had told him the previous week his grades and behavior had earned him the standard three-day Christmas pass home. He would be leaving Christmas Eve morning with the other guys who had earned a trip home. Julius couldn't stop talking about how excited he was to see his mom. Ten of the twelve boys had earned a pass, but only seven of them were taking it. Three of the guys who had earned it were more content to stay at the ranch than see their families. Sergio and another guy from his cabin were the only ones who hadn't earned a pass home. As Julius was leaving the gym, he saw Sergio coming out of Troy's office.

Julius asked, "What's up, Sergio?"

Sergio jumped and nervously said, "Oh, hey Julius. I was just, uh, looking for Troy."

Julius could tell something was up. He asked, "Is everything ok?"

Sergio nervously answered, "Yeah, bro. It's all good. Catch you later."

Sergio rushed off down the hall.

Julius didn't know what Sergio was up to, but he had a bad feeling about it.

Julius showered and got ready for dinner.

After they ate they were washing the dishes and Troy abruptly called them all together. They quickly gathered in the main room.

He said very sternly, "I know someone has broken into my office and stolen the extra set of keys to the van. That tells me someone, or a few of you, want to make a run for it. We'll deal with why you're making such an incredibly stupid decision later. Right now, I want the person or people responsible to tell me who you are and return the keys. Otherwise all Christmas break trips will be immediately cancelled. Also, the New Year's Party with the girls will be cancelled. It will get much worse from there if someone doesn't take responsibility within the next fifteen minutes."

All the guys looked around at one another. Julius knew it was Sergio who had taken the keys. Troy and TJ left the room.

Jamal asked aloud, "So, who's the idiot?"

Kerry begged, "Come on guys. I really want to see my family for Christmas!"

Sebastian said, "Are you kidding me? Stealing Troy's keys? Real smart!"

Several of the guys got up and gathered in loud groups discussing their situation.

Julius went over to Sergio who was standing in a corner alone. Julius said, "Man, we both know you took those keys. You got to own this."

Sergio replied, "What are you, a snitch? Keep your mouth shut. You don't know anything."

Julius said, "Man, you're hurting everyone here. And I know you took them!"

Sergio answered, "Well, where are they then? If you snitch it's going to be worse than whatever Troy dishes out."

Julius said, "I'm not so sure about that. I think Troy could bring some pain. You do the right thing. I know you're better than this."

Sergio said, "You don't know nothin' about me, man. Nothin'!"

He said, "Sergio, I know there's hope for you, even if you don't."

TJ exploded into the room, "Everybody sit down! I hope someone takes responsibility for this right now, or it's going to be a long, bad night for every one of you!"

Troy followed him into the room as the guys were seated.

Troy calmly said, "Your fifteen minutes are almost up. Punishments will increase dramatically at that time. I won't physically harm you, that's not what we're ever about. It's fifteen degrees outside tonight. Moving piles of wood out in this cold weather all night won't be fun."

The room was dead silent.

Troy looked at his watch and said, "Three seconds, two, one...."

Julius raised his hand. Sergio gritted his teeth and clinched his fist.

Troy asked, "Julius, you have something to say?"

Julius answered, "Yes, sir."

He looked over at Sergio and then back to Troy.

He said, "I take responsibility for stealing the keys."

Troy looked at him unbelievingly and asked, "Julius, you're saying you stole the van keys from my office?"

Julius said, "That's not what I said or what you asked for. You asked for someone to take responsibility. I am taking it."

Troy paused and then said, "That's noble of you, Julius, but it's no help without the van keys. Whoever took them must return them."

Julius said, "Check above the ceiling tile in the bathroom of the other guys cabin. I think you'll find them there."

Troy looked over at TJ. He left the room. A few minutes later he returned holding the stolen keys.

Troy took them and looked down at the keys in his hands.

He said, "Julius, your Christmas break pass is revoked. You will do extra chores daily for one month. Now, everyone get to your cabins. Game time is cancelled. Lights out in ten minutes. And I don't want to hear a sound out of any of you! Move!"

The boys got out of there quickly. Outside, Sergio walked up to Julius and asked, "How did you know where I put those keys?"

Julius turned to him and said flatly, "I was a thief too, Sergio. Putting them anywhere in your belongings would have gotten you caught. Same thing if you hid them under your mattress, in your pillow case or in the ceiling tile above your bed. It's too cold outside to bury them and you're too lazy to put much effort into hiding them very far away."

Sergio stared at Julius in amazement. He asked, "Why didn't you just turn me in?"

Julius said, "No sense in everyone suffering because of your selfishness. Anyway, Jesus took my punishment which is a lot bigger deal than what I'm doing. I believe there's hope for you, Sergio. Even if you don't. Looks like we'll be spending Christmas together."

Julius turned and walked to his cabin.

Sergio was shocked as he felt his eyes uncharacteristically well-up with tears. No one had ever actually cared enough to sacrifice for him.

Chapter 19

The next morning was Christmas Eve. It was Julius' eighteenth birthday today. He laid in his bed thinking about how much he missed his mom and friends from church. He reflected on last night's events and how several of the guys thanked him for taking responsibility, even though they knew he was innocent. He saved them from all getting their passes cancelled.

Alarms started going off and guys began getting up and ready. Chores still had to be done this morning and breakfast made before anyone left for their Christmas break.

Everyone was eating when Troy came down the hall from his office. He said, "Julius Williams, come with me."

Julius got up and followed Troy back to his office. They sat down and faced one another across Troy's desk.

He said, "Julius, everyone in this camp knows Sergio took those keys. We also know Sergio constantly tries to get you in trouble. Why in the world did you take responsibility for what he did?"

Julius answered, "It's better for one guy to take the punishment for everyone than for all to suffer. In a way, I think it's what Jesus did for us. Not that I'm anything near as good as Him. But didn't He get punished for sins He didn't commit? Even though I'm disappointed, I can handle it. Those other guys don't deserve to miss seeing their families."

Troy said, "Well, the only way for you to get on the van this morning and go to the bus station is if you tell me Sergio took the keys, or if he admits to it himself. I don't want to see you miss your visit home. Would you like to change your story?"

Julius took in a deep breath and then said, "I take the responsibility and the punishment for the stolen keys."

Troy said, "Well then, it's a good thing for you Sergio came to me early this morning and admitted to stealing them."

Julius exclaimed, "What?"

Troy said, "That's right! Sergio said he felt guilty you had taken the rap for this. He was upset by not earning a Christmas pass home. He was going to either make a run for it or get everyone else's passes revoked. His plan was working until you took the blame. He said he wants to know the God that you serve because he's never seen anyone care about others the way you did last night."

Julius said, "Sergio got saved?"

Troy smiled and said, "Best Christmas gift anyone can get! Julius, you are right. Your actions were a small picture of what Christ did for us. He was innocent and pure. He took the wrath that was meant for us, so we can become children of God. We can never earn that gift, but we can only acknowledge it freely when the Holy Spirit opens our eyes to the truth. Sergio acknowledged Jesus as his Savior early this morning!"

Julius smiled, "That's the best news you could have given me!"

Troy replied, "I guess the second best news is you better get packed. You're going home!"

When Julius came back down the hall he walked into the main room and all the guys, minus Sergio, were standing around a birthday cake with eighteen candles. They all began singing "Happy Birthday" to Julius. He walked over and blew out the candles.

Max said, "You didn't make a wish, Bro."

Julius answered, "Don't need to. All my wishes are already being answered by God!"

They all ate cake and celebrated.

The guys who were headed home for Christmas gathered together with their bags in the main cabin. Troy was pulling the van around to load them up to go to the Kingsland bus station. Sergio entered the building to start on some of his extra chores. Julius walked over to him.

They silently stared at one another.

Julius broke the silence, "Man, thank you for owning up to what you did."

Sergio replied, "No problem. I did the crime, I should do the time. That was something else last night. I have never seen anyone sacrificing for a group like you did."

Julius answered, "Jesus did a lot more sacrificing than I ever thought about. I hear you're a believer now. True story? Or are you hoping Troy won't punish you if you say you're a Christian?"

Sergio smiled and said, "Man, you know Troy. He's gonna tear me down for pulling that stunt regardless of what I say or do. But he'll turn around and build me back up. He's awesome. It's true. God opened my eyes last night to who I really was. I think seeing how Troy, TJ, you, and Max are always so consistent in how you treat others helped me see that Jesus really loves me. It won't be easy, but I want to change."

Julius said, "Brother, I will help you all I can."

Sergio replied, "I'm looking forward to it."

Julius said, "Looks like Troy's ready for us to load up. I'll see you in a few days. You stay strong because when I get back it's on!"

Sergio and Julius fist bumped.

Julius opened up his arms wide and said, "Bring it in for the real thing."

They hugged it out.

Former nemesis, now fellow brothers in Christ.

Chapter 20

On the bus ride home, Julius reflected on his time at the Second Chance Ranch. He had grown stronger spiritually, physically, emotionally, and mentally. Although he had originally dreaded going there, he now realized God knew what was best for him. He had learned a lot from Troy. The bus came to a stop and Julius grabbed his duffel bag. He stepped off the bus and was amazed at what he saw.

The small bus station was overflowing with people from New Hope Church. There was a large banner that read, "Happy Birthday and Merry Christmas, Julius!" Several people were holding signs welcoming him home. In the front of the crowd was his mom, Wanda Williams. He jumped off the bus and ran to her. Everyone cheered! They all broke out into singing, "Happy Birthday." Julius hugged and spoke to the people all around him. He couldn't believe the love his church had for him. Finally, Victor calmed the crowd down and exclaimed, "Julius Williams...Welcome home! Happy Birthday and Merry Christmas!"

Julius smiled and thanked everyone. His mom eventually took him home. He was so happy. She had made him a birthday cake and wanted to hear all about what he had been doing and learning. He spent the afternoon telling her about it. She was so proud of him.

They got ready to go to the ten o'clock Christmas Eve service at New Hope Church. They had services at six and ten o'clock because of all the new members. Each person was handed a candle when they entered the church. It was dimly but beautifully lit throughout. The service opened with a touching Christmas video about Jesus being the reason for the season. The Christmas Choir then broke into holiday songs of praise. A young man Julius remembered from the great Redemption Park revival came forward with his wife. Sky Burleson played his guitar while his wife beautifully sang "Mary, Did You Know?"

Next, Victor called all the children to the front and read the Christmas story from the book of Luke. Victor read how Joseph and Mary had to travel to Bethlehem to take part in a census to be taxed. Because there were so many people there, they couldn't find a place to stay. They ended up staying in a stable where animals were kept. He read about angels proclaiming the coming of the Savior, Jesus. Victor shared how royalty didn't come to visit the King of Kings on the night He was born, but poor shepherds did. When he was done, the kids went back and sat with their parents. Someone began playing "Silent Night" softly on the piano.

Victor lit his candle from the one on the stage. Then he lit someone else's candle at the front of the room. Soon candles were lit all around the room and everyone joined in singing together.

After the service, Julius spoke with Sky and Chloe for a little bit. They said their prayer team at Big Oak Christian Church had been praying for him every day since he had been at the ranch. He was amazed people he barely knew were concerned enough to spend time in prayer for him. They shared how their Pastor, Patrick Spakes, felt the Holy Spirit telling him Julius would someday become a great man of God who would influence many to follow Christ. Julius was humbled.

After speaking with the Burleson's, Julius caught up with Victor and Hector.

Hector said, "Merry Christmas, Julius!"

Julius replied, "Merry Christmas to you too."

Victor said, "Julius, looks like you are in even better shape than when you left. You must be working hard at the ranch. We might have to send Hector back with you!"

Hector said, "Hey Cuz, I'm gaining sympathy weight with Elizabeth. It's normal during a pregnancy. Looks like you've put on a pound or two yourself!"

Victor smiled and said, "You're absolutely right, Hector. My New Year's resolution is to lose a few pounds."

Hector answered, "Yeah, that's original!"

The guys laughed.

Victor said, "Julius, I'm looking forward to you and your mom coming for Christmas supper tomorrow evening. We're going to have a special guest with us."

Julius said, "I can't wait! Who is it?"

Hector said, "Me! I'll be there and I'm special!"

Victor said, "Yes, you are Hector. In a variety of ways. But someone else will also be there I'm sure you'll want to see. We'll keep it a surprise for now."

Julius said, "Okay, Pastor Vic. Man it's good to be home! But the ranch has been the best thing for me the past few months. I have a lot to tell you about tomorrow."

Victor said, "I'm excited to hear all about it. See you tomorrow. Happy Birthday and Merry Christmas."

Julius said, "Merry Christmas back at ya!"

He caught up with his mom and headed home.

Julius lay in bed thinking about how incredible the day had been. It had started with him thinking he wasn't going to get to come home. Shortly thereafter he learned the miraculous news of Sergio's salvation. The scene at the bus station was marvelous. So much love was shown to him on his arrival back to Westside. He thought about the special Christmas Eve service and how good it was being back home.

As wonderful as it was being here with his mom, Julius let his mind wander back to the ranch. He prayed for Sergio and for Troy. He prayed for TJ, Max, and Jamal. Julius realized he missed being with his friends in the place where Jesus was growing him. He would be ready to get back to his training.

Chapter 21

Christmas morning Julius woke up at six a.m. He got out of bed and walked into the kitchen where his mom was reading her Bible.

He leaned down, gave her a kiss and said, "Good morning, Mama. Merry Christmas!"

She replied, "Good morning, baby. Merry Christmas to you too. Could you not sleep well?"

Julius answered, "I slept great. I'm just used to getting up early every day at the ranch. I'm just happy I don't have to go outside in the cold to gather the chicken eggs this morning."

She laughed, "I never dreamed I'd hear those words come out of your mouth. My boy gathering fresh eggs. Sounds like something your grandpa would tell us about."

Julius said, "I remember some of those stories, when I was a little kid, before he passed. Mom, I'm sorry for the things I've put you through."

Wanda reached over and took his hand and said, "Honey, that's all in the past. I'm so proud of you and the man you are becoming. I can see a big difference in you."

Julius said, "Thanks, Mama. I love you so much. You have always been here for me. I know it hasn't been easy."

Wanda replied, "No, it hasn't. But it's been worth it. Now, let me make you a big Christmas breakfast."

Julius said, "No way! I haven't been able to get you a present. So my gift to you is cooking breakfast for you this morning!"

Wanda teared up and said, "Having my baby home is the best present I could ever get."

Around noon, Dwayne and Theresa picked Julius up to go for a ride and catch up. As they showed him around town he was amazed by all the changes. Mayor White had begun a renovation of downtown Westside and it looked like all the buildings were getting a facelift. Several churches had volunteers constantly doing clean-up projects and other towns were sending in teams to help as well. The 3t Challenge spurred many people into action searching for ways to invest their time, talents, and treasures serving others in the name of Jesus.

Dwayne pointed out a building downtown that housed a new job training office. A man from Big Oak Christian Church in Lost Creek was paying the rent for New Hope Church members to train and assist people who wanted to improve their job skills or simply find a job. They helped people write their resumes and fill out job application forms. They also taught basic computer skills. This helped a lot of people get jobs and move up to better ones.

They drove down to Redemption Park and it looked completely different than Julius remembered. There was a new sign and the park was very clean. Theresa told him how in the spring they were going to plant flowers all over the park. Dwayne pointed out the new playground and where the new basketball and tennis courts would be. They were also developing a scenic walking trail with vastly improved security.

As they drove, Julius saw some construction equipment just outside of downtown. Dwayne said he heard Mayor White had convinced a big manufacturer to build a new facility there. With the recent drop in crime and the overhauling of the downtown district, the company saw Westside as a good location. It would hire one hundred and seventy-five people from the area. That would be a big boost to the local economy.

Julius told them about his experiences at the ranch. Dwayne and Theresa shared about everything God was doing in their lives. Although they hadn't known Julius very long before he was sent away, they had quickly become close friends. They prayed together when they dropped Julius off at home. He went inside and got ready to go to Victor's for Christmas dinner.

Julius and his mom walked up to Victor's home with their arms full of presents. As they walked in, they could smell the sweet aroma of a delicious Christmas dinner. Everyone joyfully greeted one another. Julius noticed a table covered in pies, candy, and fudge. They placed their presents under the tree. Julius looked around and saw Victor, Maria, Hector, Elizabeth, and their son Pedro. He was curious as to who the special guest Victor had mentioned the night before would be. He thought maybe Troy had come into town or Pastor Patrick and his family might have driven in from Lost Creek.

Victor saw him looking around and asked, "What are you thinking about, Julius?"

He answered, "Nothing really. Just wondering who the special guest is that you mentioned last night."

Victor smiled, "They should be here soon. Are you having a good visit with your mom?"

Julius answered, "No. I'm having a great visit! Hey, Pastor Vic, can I get you to check into something for me?"

Victor said, "Sure. What is it?"

Julius replied, "There's something going on at the ranch. Troy won't discuss it with us, but I think they're having some kind of money problems or something. Could you look into it?"

Victor said, "Of course. I'll see what I can find out. Second Chance Ranch is such a great program. I would hate to see it go under. It's a ministry people should really support. It has a great reputation and success rate. That's the reason I wanted you to go there."

Julius said, "That's right. The guys there are really growing and becoming good men. I'm so glad God allowed me to go there instead of prison."

Outside a car door shut. A minute later there was a knock at the door and Brother Reginald walked inside. Behind him walked in Mr. Alexander!

Everyone greeted him warmly.

Mr. Alexander walked over to Julius and said, "Merry Christmas, young man. I believe I owe you a very big apology. Can you find it in your heart to forgive me for what I did in anger?"

Julius was in shock. Mr. Alexander was the last person he expected to see. He asked, "What do you mean?"

Mr. Alexander answered, "I pressed charges on you for doing something that wasn't your idea because I was angry. My son made bad decisions and involved you. I should have understood. But I was so angry I just wanted everyone to be miserable like I was. Please forgive me for being hateful."

Julius said, "What you intended for harm, God used for good. I forgive you completely."

The two guys hugged.

Mr. Alexander said, "Thank you, Julius. And thank you for the weekly letters. God used them to soften my heart, along with Pastor Victor going out of his way to care about me."

Julius said, "You've read my letters? I didn't know if you were even getting them."

He answered, "Yes, but I've only recently become a believer and follower of Jesus. Victor thought it would be fun to surprise you in person."

Victor said, "Surprise! Praise the Lord for who He is and for sending His Son. Let's gather at the table and pray before we eat. Reginald, would you please pray for us this evening?"

Reginald prayed and everyone enjoyed the great Christmas feast. They laughed and talked until everyone was done. Then they all opened presents. Julius got some new sneakers and a new basketball from his mom. Victor had picked up some perfume for Julius to give to his mom. Julius thanked him multiple times. Others got Christian books and music. Mr. Alexander gave Julius a wrapped present.

Julius opened it. In the box was a Monopoly "Get Out of Jail Free" card.

Julius looked curiously at Mr. Alexander.

He said, "Julius, I'm going to drop the charges and petition the court to drop your sentence. You will probably be home in less than a week!"

Wanda screamed and jumped up to hug Julius. Everyone cheered and clapped. Victor watched Julius closely. He could tell what was coming next, and he was happy about it.

Julius interrupted the celebration, "Thank you so much for such a gracious and forgiving offer, Mr. Alexander. But I don't want you to do that."

His mom asked, "What, Julius? Don't you want to come home?"

Julius answered, "Yes, Ma'am. I sure do. Just as soon as I finish what I started at Second Chance Ranch. I'm growing so much there and influencing a lot of guys who really need it. God has placed me there, and I don't feel like He's finished with me being there yet."

Victor said, "Julius, it sounds like you've made up your mind. Is there any doubt about your decision whatsoever?"

Julius resolutely answered, "No, sir."

Victor said, "Then we will honor your decision. I'm proud of you caring so much about others. Go finish the training and work where God has called you. Mr. Alexander, you're good with this decision?"

Mr. Alexander answered, "I'm proud of you, young man. Of course I'll honor your wishes."

Julius said, "Thank you for understanding. I haven't gotten the chance to tell everyone the story about my friend Sergio, and how he got saved yesterday. Can I tell you now?"

The rest of the evening was spent listening to Julius talk about his friends, eating desserts, and singing Christmas carols.

Chapter 22

The next morning, Julius packed up and got ready to head back to Second Chance Ranch. His mom drove him over to Hector and Elizabeth's. They had cooked a huge breakfast for everyone. Victor, Maria, Reginald, Dwayne, Theresa, Ramone, and Mia were all there. They ate, talked, and laughed for over an hour. When it was time for Julius to leave for the bus station they all laid hands on him and prayed. It was a powerful time of bold prayers for Julius to continue following Jesus and keep growing into the man God created him to be. It reminded Victor of the Apostle Paul describing how they prayed over Timothy in the New Testament.

Victor and Reginald followed them to the bus station. As they said their goodbyes, Victor couldn't help but think back to just a few months ago when Julius was first leaving. This time his leaving felt much better. Julius had grown in his faith and walk with God. He was noticeably becoming a leader. Victor was very proud of him.

Julius hugged his mom and kissed her on the cheek. Then turned to the men and said, "Thank you for everything. I really mean it. I'm excited about finishing school. The next time I see you will probably be at my graduation. God Bless!"

They watched him turn and get onto the waiting bus.

About four hours later he arrived once again at the Kingsland Bus Depot. Troy was there with Sebastian, Drake, and Jamal. They were all glad to see each other.

Troy said, "Welcome back, Julius!"

Jamal added, "Nice kicks, Bro!"

Julius smiled, "Man, Santa was good to me! Looks like you got some nice ones too."

Drake said, "Jamal keeps talking about how he can't wait to get me on the court. I don't care what kind of shoes he's got, he won't hang with me!"

Jamal laughed, "Drake, I'll beat you like Julius beats that punching bag. How was your visit home, Big Julius?"

Julius answered, "It was great! I can't believe how much the town has changed. And Troy, you're not going to believe some of the things God is doing down in Westside."

Troy said, "Well you might not believe what He's doing around here! I can't wait to catch up!"

Jamal said, "I can't wait to school all of you in some hoops this spring!"

Troy said, "Jamal, I don't need any fancy shoes to take you. I could beat you and your overpriced shoes barefooted out in the snow right now!"

All the guys busted out laughing. Julius was happy to be back. He knew this was where he was supposed to be.

The drive out to Second Chance Ranch took a little longer because of the snow. Julius felt like he was experiencing life more than ever. He noticed the beautiful glistening white landscape and snow covered pines. The sunbeams piercing through the clouds were majestic. He was learning to notice and appreciate the awesomeness of God's creation.

Once they got back to the ranch the guys got settled in their cabin. A little while later, Troy popped in and asked Julius to come with him. Julius bundled up and went outside with Troy. They walked over to an area overlooking the big pasture. Troy had built a campfire. They sat down by it and warmed themselves.

Julius asked, "What are we doing out here?"

Troy answered, "I just wanted to take a few minutes and catch up. It sounds like you had a good visit back home."

Julius said, "Yeah. It was pretty awesome. Honestly, it's amazing how so many people have invested in me and how God has blessed me. I don't deserve all of their love."

Troy said, "That's great. I can see you developing into a leader. Do you realize how much the guys here look up to you?"

Julius asked, "Really? You think?"

Troy said, "Julius, all of these guys look up to you for several reasons. Don't let this go to your head, but they follow your lead. If you want to do something, they want to do it. When you think something is funny, they do too. Leadership is influence, Julius. And you influence these guys a lot."

Julius said, "I don't guess I've ever thought about it. Why are you telling me this, Troy?"

"Because you need to know the way you live matters. Your attitude, your work ethic, your faith are all magnified because people are watching and emulating you. It's important for you to be aware of that. It's a form of power. And you know the old saying, 'With great power comes great responsibility.' Julius, you can affect lots of people for God."

Julius sat quietly for a few minutes thinking about what Troy had said.

Julius asked, "What do I do now? You're a great leader. How do I use my potential for God?"

Troy answered, "Ask Him. God will show you day by day. It's the most rewarding journey you can take!"

Julius smiled and said, "Thanks, Troy. You'll continue to help me grow won't you?"

Troy answered, "As long as I can Julius. Have you had a chance to talk to Sergio?"

Julius answered, "Not yet. How's he doing?"

Troy said, "One-hundred-eighty degree turn around. His attitude has completely changed and he's hungry to learn more about Jesus. Reminds me of you when you first got here."

Julius said, "Man, that's amazing. I had written that dude off. Guess it's a good thing God didn't."

Troy said, "You never know where the Holy Spirit is moving. I love seeing you guys wake up to the love of God. It's always amazing! Don't ever give up on anyone, Julius. You never know where the Lord might do a miracle."

Julius said, "I hear ya, Troy. Check out that sunset. Isn't God an awesome artist?"

Troy looked out at the magnificent red, orange, and yellow colors painted across the western sky.

He thoughtfully answered, "Yes, He is, Julius. Yes, He is."

Chapter 23

All the guys gathered for supper that evening. They were happy to be together again. They laughed and caught up with each other. After they had eaten, Troy told them to meet in the main room after the kitchen was cleaned.

When they were all settled in Troy said, "Several of you have been home for Christmas. The rest of us have been here at the ranch. I'd like to take this evening and give you guys the chance to catch up."

Jamal began, "I had a good visit with my mom and sister. We went over to my cousins and opened presents. That's when I got these sweet shoes. Which is what I'm gonna be wearing when I wear all of you out on the court!"

The guys all started talking trash.

Troy spoke up over them, "Okay! Okay! Settle down. Jamal, I do like those shoes. On a different note, did you get a chance to share your new faith in Jesus with your family?"

Jamal said, "Yes, I did. I told my mom and she was so happy. I also had a good talk with my little sister. She's sweet, but I can tell she's struggling. We haven't seen our dad in over eight years. It's just tough."

Troy asked, "I know we've talked about this individually, but raise your hand if your dad lives with you in your house."

Only three of the twelve guys raised their hand.

Troy continued, "Okay. Now if you know your dad, but he's in prison raise your hand."

Six of the twelve guys raised their hand.

Troy asked, "If you don't know your dad, raise your hand."

Julius, Max, and Sergio raised their hand.

Troy said, "I appreciate your honesty. Guys, as you can see absentee fatherhood is a huge problem in our society. Here's two things I want you to know about fatherhood. The first thing is God is never absent. He is always available and wants to have a relationship with you. James 4:8 begins, 'Draw near to God and He will draw near to you.' The Bible teaches God will never leave you or forsake you. God is never too busy for you.

"The other thing about fatherhood I want you to know is you can be an awesome husband and father regardless of how your dad treated you. Choose right now to be the dad you wish you had. The Bible teaches a lot about authentic manhood, which our culture has abandoned. I want you to become men who follow God and lead their families."

Troy paused to allow the guys to think about what he had said. Then he asked, "Who would like to share about the past few days next?"

Sergio said, "As many of you know, I became a follower of Jesus on Christmas Eve. The reason I wanted to know Jesus was because of the difference I saw in many of you. I'm amazed at the peace God has given me. I was full of hate. Troy explained to me how I need to ask forgiveness from those I've hurt. Not to earn my Salvation, but because I am saved. I'm sorry for picking fights with most of you and putting you down. Julius, I'm especially sorry for how I've treated you. Can you forgive me?"

Julius said, "Yeah Sergio, I totally forgive you. What you're doing right now is how I ended up here. I was asking forgiveness of people I had sinned against. There was this man, Mr. Alexander, who pressed charges against me. But you know what God did? He used that situation to lead me here. And while I was home I found out Mr. Alexander had gotten saved!"

Julius told them the whole story of his experiences at home. The other guys opened up about their experiences too. It was a great night of the group bonding together.

Later that evening, as the discussion time came to end, Troy explained the schedule for the next week. They would have to be up to do their chores and eat breakfast at the regular time. After breakfast they would still have chapel, but after it they would have free time the rest of the day. This would last for the whole break as long as there were no problems.

Troy also announced they were invited to a New Year's Eve party at the girls' camp. This was all welcome news to the boys. The anticipation of the coming week had the guys very excited as they went to their cabins.

Chapter 24

It was a special time at the ranch. The guys enjoyed having a break from studying. They got along great and really began to discuss deeper, real issues with each other. Troy was happy to see them growing together as a group.

One day as they ate lunch a truck pulled up with a big trailer behind it. The guys got excited.

Julius asked, "What's going on?"

Max replied, "Looks like it's horseback riding for this afternoon's entertainment."

Julius was nervous, "Oh, man. I don't know about riding a horse."

Jamal said, "Just embrace it, dude. Troy ain't gonna let you get out of this one."

The guys finished eating and went out to the horses. They brought six horses out of the trailer for the group to ride. Troy took volunteers for the first round. After the second group went Julius knew his time was up. Filled with trepidation, he walked over to the horses. Troy explained everything to him. Julius raised his foot up into the stirrup and hopped up onto the saddle. He was tense, but Troy led him around in a circle while he got used to everything. A few minutes later Julius was smiling and riding a horse by himself for the very first time!

As the New Year's Eve party approached they were informed the girls were having a karaoke contest along with the dance. The guys started thinking about what they wanted to sing. Some of them started working on routines together. Others were coming up with funny dances to perform with their songs. They were excited!

The big night finally arrived and the guys got ready. Troy and TJ loaded them up in the van and they drove over to the girls' camp. When they got there they went into the girls' main cabin. The girls had it all decorated. They had also prepared a big steak dinner. Everyone gathered in a circle and prayed before they sat down to eat. The counselors, Troy, TJ, Rachel, and Amber, served them dinner and everyone enjoyed eating and being together. Julius and Max sat with Heather, Katie, and Holly. The girls were obviously excited to see the guys. They talked about everything from Christmas presents to New Year's resolutions while they ate. After dinner the tables were moved out of the way and they began taking requests for karaoke songs.

Troy kicked things off with the song, "Word Up" by Cameo. Everyone was laughing and having a great time. Rachel and Amber got up next and sang, "Coal Miner's Daughter" in their most twangy voices, which was hilarious. They were having a blast.

During the evening, Max sang, "I Did It My Way", doing his best impersonation of Elvis at times. Katie and Holly sang, "Oceans" by Hillsong. Julius sang, "Ain't No Mountain High Enough" by Marvin Gaye. Jamal performed the "Macarena" which everyone made fun of at first, but they were all doing the dance in no time. Several other songs were performed solo and by multiple singers. It was a fun night.

Around eleven o'clock they started playing dance music and everyone joined in. They did line dances and at times formed two rows to dance through. Several of them were really good dancers and singers.

At eleven forty-five they all bundled up and went outside. Troy lit a bonfire and had everyone hold hands in a circle around it. He said one thing he was thankful for from the previous year. Then Rachel, who was standing to his right, said what she was thankful for. This continued around the circle until everyone had shared.

Troy checked his watch and began counting down from ten. Everyone joined in and counted down together, "Three. Two. One. Happy New Year!"

They all began hugging each other and celebrating. Julius thought he saw Troy sneak a kiss from Rachel. They were enjoying the moment when, from out of nowhere, a missile shot high into the sky and a thunderous "BOOM!" rang out! Then an assortment of rockets began launching and popping in the night sky. This surprised everyone. After the initial shock, they all began to cheer. It turned out, TJ had set up a huge fireworks show for the kids. They loved it!

This would be a New Year's celebration they would remember for the rest of their lives.

Chapter 25

Early the next morning Julius went over to the gym in the main cabin. He couldn't sleep late even though Troy had given everyone permission to sleep in after the late night. As Julius finished his workout he walked by Troy's office. The door was cracked open, and as he walked by he heard Troy say, "I understand we are a little behind on our payments. We're doing our best to catch up with those bills."

It must have been on speaker, because Julius could hear another voice as well.

The stranger said, "Troy, this is a courtesy call. We've toured the ranch and we want it to succeed. You and the ranch's board came to us for this loan. We are a bank, not a charity."

Troy said, "I understand that, sir. We ARE a charity and a lot of our donors have quit giving. We're adjusting our finances and plan to catch up with our payments soon."

The stranger said, "I certainly hope so. If you haven't caught up by the end of this month, we're going to have to foreclose on the ranch. I'm sorry."

Troy answered, "I understand. We'll be caught up by then somehow. I assure you."

The stranger said, "I certainly hope so. Goodbye."

Julius silently made his way to the end of the hallway. As he stepped into the main room he heard Troy's voice behind him say, "Julius, what are you doing up this early?"

Julius turned around, "Just getting in a workout. Wanted to start the year right."

Troy said, "Come here."

Julius slowly walked back into Troy's office.

Troy reached onto his desk and grabbed an envelope. "You got some mail. I was going to drop it off later."

Julius took it. "Thanks."

Troy answered, "Yeah. Go get cleaned up. We'll have breakfast in a little while."

Julius said, "Yes, sir."

As he started to exit Troy said, "Hey, Julius."

He froze.

Troy continued, "Pray for our camp. God is growing us through some interesting times right now."

Julius, realizing he hadn't been caught eavesdropping, answered, "Always. Troy, thank you for everything you do. I know it's not easy."

Troy had a blank look on his face. "Thanks. That means more than you know, Julius. Go get cleaned up."

Julius got back to his cabin. Some of the guys were slowly moving around. Julius looked at the return address and knew this was a letter from his mom. He sat down on his bunk and opened it up. He read,

"*Julius,*

It was so good to have you home for Christmas. I'm so proud of you and the man you are becoming. I couldn't have asked for a better Christmas present than spending it with my son. Everyone has been going on about how mature you are now.

Julius, I realize not knowing your dad has always been tough on you. Especially when you hit your teenage years. I've prayed long and hard about what I'm about to tell you. Your father's real name is Cecil Williams. We always laughed about already having the same last name. He would say it's like we were already married. We met when I was only seventeen. I was infatuated with him. He was a big, strong, and very handsome man. I believe he cared about me. We dated for a year and then I became pregnant. He said he wanted to marry me and have a family. I'm not sure if it was true or not. He did bad things, Julius. He was a drunk and a thief. Shortly after he found out I was pregnant, he began beating up on me. I got away from him. He moved off and I lost contact with him. From what I understand, one night he had been drinking heavily and robbed a guy at gun point. The guy fought back and your father shot and killed him. Julius, your father is serving a life sentence in federal prison for murder. I'm sorry to have to tell you this. Honestly, I only found out where he was a few years ago. Do whatever you want with this information. I feel like you are old enough to know the truth. I love you with all my heart.

Love Always,

Mom."

Julius sat there holding the letter in shock.

Chapter 26

The rest of the month was filled with heart wrenching prayer. Troy was begging God to save the ranch. Julius was also petitioning the Lord to provide for the ranch, as well as praying for guidance on what to do with the information about his father.

Each of these men spent countless hours on their face, begging God to hear their prayers and meet their needs. They didn't realize it but God was using this time to grow them into prayer warriors.

On January 31st Troy gathered all the guys together.

He said, "Men, Second Chance Ranch has been struggling financially. We've had several churches slowly stop giving over the past few years. I've adjusted as much as possible, but it has not been enough. It takes a lot to run a ministry like this. I've gotten several phone calls threatening to foreclose on the ranch, the latest coming just this morning."

Julius felt like he had been punched in the gut. Where was God in all this?

Troy continued, "A few minutes ago I was in my office trying to figure out how to explain to you the ranch would be closing. We just didn't have the resources to continue operating. Then, I got another phone call. I just got off the phone with a man named Sky Burleson. He's a young man who attends Big Oak Christian Church in Lost Creek. He informed me our need was made known to people in churches all around the capital city, in Lost Creek, and in Westside. This afternoon a check is being sent to our lender to cover all of the back payments and penalties we are behind on paying!"

The guys clapped and cheered, but Julius knew they didn't really understand how close the ranch was to closing. They didn't totally get how faithful God had been in all of this. Julius smiled, learning the lesson first hand that leaders sometimes have to know and do more than others. He also learned that God is faithful.

Troy continued, "Sky said he and his wife, Chloe, want to come up and celebrate with us. I think we should invite the girls' camp over for the concert. Do you guys think we should invite them?"

The boys enthusiastically all yelled, "Yes!"

That afternoon Julius noticed Troy and TJ talking. They smiled, shook hands and Troy took off in the van. Julius walked over to TJ.

He asked, "Where's Troy headed?"
TJ answered, "He's got important stuff to take care of. Let's get this place looking good. Tonight's going to be a big night!"
Julius said, "Big night? What do you mean?"
TJ smiled, "Life changing, Julius. Come on, let's get to work."
Julius was intrigued.

A little while later the girls arrived. TJ had gotten the white Christmas lights out and had the guys string them along the ceiling in the main cabin. They set up an area for Sky and Chloe to perform and put white covers on all of the tables. TJ even had some of the guys bring in freshly cut evergreen branches to decorate the tables. It looked and smelled amazing.
The guys welcomed the girls. They were all excited about seeing each other. The girls loved the decorations.
Holly came up to Julius and said, "You boys outdid yourselves. This place looks exquisite. So romantic."
Julius replied, "I don't know about romantic, but it looks cool. Very clean and neat."
Max walked up, "Clean and neat? Julius, you wouldn't know romance if Romeo and Juliet were standing here talking to you."
Julius asked, "Didn't they both kill themselves?"
Holly said, "I see what you mean, Max!"
They laughed. Julius saw Sky and excused himself.
Julius walked over to him and said, "Hey! I'm not sure if you remember me..."
Sky interrupted, "Of course I remember you, Julius! Good to see you again."
He answered, "You too. How are things with Pastor Patrick and Big Oak?"
Sky said, "Things are going great! We're really experiencing God in some incredible ways. Oh, Pastor Patrick said to be sure to tell you he is proud of you and to keep following Jesus!"
He smiled, "Cool. Tell him I will."
Troy announced, "Can I have everyone's attention? I'd like to welcome Sky and Chloe Burleson to our Second Chance Ranch."
Everyone clapped.
Troy continued. "Let's all join hands and pray."

After prayer, they ate and enjoyed each other's company. Sky and Chloe set up to perform after supper.

Sky proclaimed, "It's an honor to be here tonight. We were very blessed to be able to pay off some of the bills for Second Chance Ranch today. TJ, Rachel, and Amber are some awesome counselors and Troy is a top notch director for the ranch. You know this better than me though!"

The kids cheered.

Sky continued, "Many people can't give up their time to be here for you, but they sacrificed some of their treasures for you. They gave their money, so you can have a safe place to grow and learn. But these four counselors are sacrificing their very lives to love you and help you succeed in life. Don't ever take the opportunity you have to be here and learn from these great leaders for granted. I'm excited to be able to hang out with all of you tonight! Who's ready for some music?"

The kids went crazy.

Sky and Chloe began with the song "Undignified." They sang several more upbeat fun songs. Some were motion songs the kids really enjoyed. They then transitioned into a time of passionate worship music. Sky finished the set and said a short prayer. Then he said, "I've had a special request tonight. You can all have a seat. This is a song called 'I Will Be Here' by Steven Curtis Chapman."

He began the song and about halfway through it Troy went over and took Rachel's hand and led her to the front of the assembly. She was shocked. He took her into his arms and they slowly danced in front of the group. Julius, as well as all the campers, knew this was highly unusual. Troy had never openly shown any affection toward Rachel, other than the New Year's Eve kiss Julius saw him sneak.

At the end of the song everyone stood and clapped. Some of the guys whistled.

Troy turned and told them all to have a seat. They did.

Troy then turned to Rachel and said, "Rachel, you are the love of my life. I thank God every day for allowing me to find you. We have been counselors here at the ranch for three years together. They have been the best days of my life."

Rachel was smiling and crying by this time.

Troy pulled a ring from his pocket. He dropped to one knee and said, "Rachel McKinney, would you do me the honor of becoming my wife?"

Rachel, crying heavily, nodded her head and said, "Yes!" Everyone cheered!

Chapter 27

It was 10:09 p.m. on April 24th, exactly one month before the babies' due-date. Maria's morning sickness had subsided shortly after the scare last November. Since then her pregnancy had gone much better. She was actually able to enjoy it, unlike her first trimester. Victor was finishing up a call with Troy Speer at Second Chance Ranch.

He came into the room and Maria asked, "How is Julius doing?"

Victor answered, "He's doing great! He did well on his latest ACT exam. He'll graduate next month, no problem. He should also have all nine college credits he's taking."

She asked, "Do you think he will go to college?"

Victor replied, "I don't know. But, at least he's eligible if he decides to. Troy said the ranch got the check we sent. It covers the last of their bills for this year's budget!"

Maria said, "Praise the Lord. I'm so glad you connected with him after Julius told you about their financial problems."

Victor said, "Yes. Last January when we found out about it, they were really in dire straits. I'm so proud of all the churches in the capital city, Lost Creek, Westside, and all around rallying to save the ranch. Troy said he's paid back all of last year's shortfall and should be debt free by this summer on the property."

Maria asked, "Isn't the ranch paid for already?"

Victor answered, "Partially. The land and boys and girls ranches are already paid off. They have been for a while. It was the new family area they still had a bank note on. Between that and paying for feeding the kids, providing weekly psychologists, health care, school curriculum, and uniforms they were spending too much. Troy had cut his own salary, which was already very small, to keep things going."

Maria said, "It's so amazing how people who are already sacrificing continue to give when needed."

Victor continued, "Yes, it is. He definitely has a servant's heart. Unfortunately, the number of churches who had supported them in the past had dwindled. Troy was telling me how wonderful it is to have all these new and renewed relationships with so many churches. Because of this, many of them are going to send volunteers on a regular basis to invest in the kids. He's even sitting down with the Second Chance Ranch board and discussing a new area to develop on the property for church camps. He's got some great ideas about how to set it up and make it profitable to pay for upkeep on the ranch itself."

She said, "That sounds exciting! How wonderful would it be to take a group of our youth out there for a week in the summer?"

Victor agreed. He went to brush his teeth and get ready for bed. While he was brushing his teeth, he heard Maria scream! He rushed into their bedroom.

She exclaimed, "Victor, it's time!"

He sprang into action. He helped her get out of bed and to the car. He rushed back into the house and grabbed his "go bag." It was a suitcase he had prepared for this situation. On the way to the hospital he alerted Hector, who in turn triggered the New Hope prayer chain.

They rushed Maria back to Labor and Delivery. Victor parked the car and sprinted back to be with her. At eleven-thirty on April 24th, Victor and Maria Martinez became the proud parents of twin girls. They named them Daniela and Gabriela.

Hector and Elizabeth were there soon after the babies were born. They were incredibly happy and took lots of pictures. Everyone was enjoying themselves when Elizabeth exclaimed, "Hector! I think it's my turn!"

Hector asked, "What?"

Elizabeth answered, "Hector, get the nurse, our baby is coming!"

They rushed Elizabeth back to a delivery room. About two hours later she had a handsome baby boy. They named him Pablo.

She was in the room next door to Maria. Joy filled both families as they celebrated their new arrivals.

Chapter 28

The next morning several New Hope members stopped by to share their congratulations. Both families were filled with joy. Ramone Johnson and his wife Mia had already visited Victor and Maria and were now seeing Hector and Elizabeth.

After washing her hands, Mia asked, "May I hold him?"

Elizabeth answered, "Of course!" She kissed him on the head and handed him to Mia.

She said, "What a cute little boy. He has so much hair. Are you feeling okay, Elizabeth?"

Elizabeth answered, "I took a cat nap earlier. I'll be fine."

Hector asked, "Are you not worried about me? I did all the work! I kept telling Elizabeth to breath all during the delivery."

Ramone said, "He's right. Without Hector, she probably would have forgotten to breath and suffocated! He deserves a prize."

Mia, cuddling the baby in her arms, lovingly said, "He's got a wonderful little prize right here."

Hector replied, "Ramone, you better watch out. I think someone is going to want a prize of her own soon."

Ramone laughingly said, "Not until I finish seminary!"

Hector asked, "How much longer have you got to go?"

He replied, "After next month, only one more year. I'm really enjoying this semester. I have the best Systematic Theology teacher."

Mia looked intently at the baby in her arms. She sat up straight and exclaimed, "Something is wrong! He's turning blue! Call somebody! Get help now!"

Hector grabbed his son from Mia! Ramone opened the door and yelled, "We need help in here! Now!"

Two nurses rushed in and grabbed the baby from Hector. They called a code blue and other workers rushed into the room. Health care workers were all around. One nurse told Ramone and Mia to step outside the room. Hector was holding Elizabeth who was crying out, "What's wrong with him? What's going on?"

It was chaos! Then they rushed the baby out of the room, leaving Hector and Elizabeth sitting there all alone. Elizabeth burst into tears. Hector held her tight.

A little while later a nurse entered their room. She said, "Pablo is stable. My name is Janice. I'm the nurse taking care of him."

Elizabeth said, "Oh, thank God!"

Hector sighed a breath of relief.

Janice continued, "His blood is too thick for his little heart to pump. We're going to move him to the Neonatal ICU. He'll have his blood thinned out and hopefully in a few days his body will adjust and everything should be fine. We're going to get him all situated down there and then let you come visit him. Does that sound good?"

Hector said, "Yes. Please take good care of him."

Janice replied, "We have great doctors and nurses here. We will give him our very best."

Elizabeth said, "Thank you."

Janice smiled and took Elizabeth's hand. She asked, "May I pray with you?"

Elizabeth began to softly cry. She answered, "Please do."

Janice prayed for Elizabeth, Hector, and baby Pablo. This meant so much to them.

A few hours later Janice loaded Elizabeth into a wheelchair and Hector pushed her down to the NICU unit. Janice showed them where to wash their hands. Then she gave them some yellow gowns to wear over their cloths. Following Janice, they entered the NICU through a security door.

There were eight babies in this unit. As they made their way down the row, Hector noticed how tiny most of them were. Some were as small as one or two pounds. They were lying in clear plastic cases with lights covering them. There were little wires and tubes running into the cases connected to the babies. They made their way to the very last unit in the corner. There was a blue card with the words 'Baby Gonzales' written on it in black. Pablo looked like a giant compared to the other babies in there. He had an IV placed in the top of his little head.

Janice explained, "We weren't able to get an IV started in his arms or legs. I know it looks bad, but it really doesn't hurt him. You can hold him a little later. He's been through a lot and is resting right now."

Hector said, "His color looks good. Is he pumping his blood better now?"

Janice answered, "Yes! The medicine has thinned his blood and he's doing fine. I'll let you have some privacy. Take all the time you want. Let me know if you need anything."

Elizabeth asked, "How long does he have to stay in here?"

Janice answered, "At least a few days. The doctor will be by your room in a little while to update you. We'll take very good care of him until we can get him back to his mommy. I know this is tough. Hang in there."

Hector and Elizabeth held hands as they stood there and prayed for their little baby.

Chapter 29

The next few days were hard for Elizabeth. Maria and Victor visited Hector and Elizabeth's room regularly. Maria and the twins were discharged three days after their birth. It was unusual for twins to go home this soon, but they were doing great. Insurance would only pay for Elizabeth staying in the hospital for three days. Pablo was still in NICU, but the doctors said he was responding well.

Hector and Elizabeth had to go home without their baby. Hector's parents had been taking care of Pedro. They said they would keep him a few more days so Hector and Elizabeth could rest. Elizabeth was silent on the drive home. When they arrived, Hector walked her into the house. He went back to the car to grab their bags and brought them inside and put them away. Hector walked through the house, but didn't find Elizabeth. He walked down the hall to the baby's room and pushed open the door. Elizabeth was sitting in her rocking chair crying. Hector didn't know what to say. He put his hand on her shoulder and said, "I love you."

She reached up and placed her hand on top of his and patted it. She said, "I know. Thank you."

As hard as it was for him, Hector had no idea how tough it would be for a mom to come home without her baby.

The next morning they went to the hospital and visited Pablo. The doctor said he looked good and should go home in about two more days. His blood was naturally thinning itself now. Elizabeth and Hector almost felt guilty for being upset, as they looked at all the other babies in the unit. Pablo was two or three times the size of most of them. They were able to hold him and get pictures. Fortunately, the IV in his head had been removed. They laughed as they were taking pictures holding him. Elizabeth felt better. She wanted to stay a while and just hold Pablo. Hector went downstairs to get a snack.

As Elizabeth rocked little Pablo, she noticed a young girl had come into the unit. She stood by her tiny baby's clear case staring at her as the nurse talked. After the nurse stepped away, she began to cry. Elizabeth put Pablo back in his crib and walked down to the young lady.

She softly said, "Hi. I'm Elizabeth. Is this your baby?"

The young mom replied, "Yes. Her name is Shonda Hansberry Lee."

Elizabeth observed, "That's a pretty name. She's a beautiful little girl."

The young mom said through red teary eyes, "Thank you. I'm Tamica. I think she's the most beautiful thing I've ever seen. I just wish I could have carried her full term so she wouldn't be so sick. I hate seeing her with all those tubes and wires in her little body."

Elizabeth said, "I know how you feel. My son is right down there."

Tamica asked, "How is he?"

Elizabeth answered, "He tried to die shortly after he was born. But the doctors saved him. Just like they're going to save Shonda."

Tamica smiled and said, "I sure hope so. Her daddy ran off when he found out I was pregnant. My family is ashamed of me. I have some friends I've been staying with, but they don't want a baby around. So, I'm pretty much on my own now."

Elizabeth took Tamica's hand and said, "No, you're not. Not anymore."

Two days later Hector and Elizabeth brought Pablo home! They were so happy. As a precaution, he had to be hooked up to a monitor when he slept, but he was healthy in every way. They still went up to the hospital regularly to visit Tamica. New Hope church members joined them in praying for Tamica and visiting her consistently. She felt the love of God through their kindness.

The time spent with Tamica inspired Elizabeth. Over the next month, she began putting together a plan to help other moms who were in crisis pregnancies. She had Victor contact other pastors who had a heart for these women. Her plan was to develop a safe place where these girls could live, receive care, and deliver healthy babies.

Chapter 30

On the Friday night before graduation, Troy was setting up a big celebration party for the graduating seniors. It was now mid-May and the weather was great. He had ribs cooking, music on the back deck, and the girls' camp was coming over. There were five guys and six girls graduating the next day. It was the largest graduating class in the Second Chance Ranch's history. Everyone was excited.

Troy caught up with Julius a few hours before the party.

He said, "Hey, Julius! Are you ready for the big day tomorrow?"

Julius replied, "Yeah, I guess so."

Troy asked, "What's up? I figured you would be pumped about graduating."

He answered, "Oh, I am. That's not it. I guess I'm just sad my time here is almost up. This ranch has helped me grow so much. I'm such a better person than I ever thought I would be."

Troy thought for a moment. "Can I tell you something? Just between you and me?"

Julius answered, "Yes, sir. Just between us."

Troy said, "I'm not sure how much of my story you know. When I was sixteen, I made some bad decisions and ended up on the wrong side of the law. I got sent here. Just like you, Julius, this is where I became a man. There was a counselor here who invested in me and I responded to his tough love. I graduated in the same church you're going to be graduating in tomorrow. I went on to college and got my teaching and counseling degrees. Then I came right back here. We've had some really good students come through here, but this is by far the best year we've had since I've been a counselor. Julius, remember the talk we had after Christmas about you stepping up and becoming a leader? I know you are the reason this class has turned out so well."

Julius was surprised, "You think so? I just tried to be who God wanted me to be."

Troy said, "Exactly! And because you humbly followed Him, He used you to break down barriers in these guys lives. It's been awesome watching God not only growing you, but using you to impact these other guys. And because they saw you applying what I was teaching, I became a lot more effective in helping them grow into men."

Julius said, "It's been awesome being a part of it. But I think you're giving me too much credit. Troy, you are the one who inspired me and the guys to become more than we thought we ever could be. You have lived out what real manhood should look like. Even getting the girl. Did you and Rachel date before you got to the ranch?"

Troy smiled, "Three years ago I agreed to a five year contract here. That same year, Rachel did the same thing at the girls' ranch. We had never met. When I signed the contract, I figured I wouldn't get married until after it was up and I could get back out into the real world. God brought us together out here in the middle of nowhere. He is truly awesome."

Julius replied, "Wow! That is amazing."

Troy said, "Julius, I filled out all the paperwork with the state judicial system. Your record will be wiped totally clean as of tomorrow when you graduate. There will be no record of any crimes in your adult file. Fresh start."

Julius just smiled.

Troy said, "Okay. I have to check on those ribs."

Julius said, "Thanks for sharing all of this with me, Troy. I'm glad God allowed us to cross paths."

Troy answered, "Me too, Julius. Let me pray for us and then let's get this place ready for a party."

The two men bowed down on their knees and spent some time praising and thanking God.

Julius was walking over to his cabin when he ran into Max and Sergio. He could tell they were talking about something serious.

He asked, "What's up fella's?"

Max answered, "We're just trying to figure out what's next."

Julius asked, "What do you mean?"

Sergio explained, "Julius, tomorrow after graduation, you're headed home to move back in with your mom. We all know that. But Max and I want to do something different than move back home. My home life was terrible and, honestly, I'm not sure if my mom even wants me back there."

Max said, "My mom wouldn't mind if I moved back in, but I think God is leading me somewhere else. I just don't know where. I know it's not to the foreign mission field, but I don't think it's back home either."

Jamal walked up, "What's this meeting of the mind's about?"

Julius said, "We're talking about what we'll do after we graduate. There's a lot going on in Westside. And it's close to the capital city. Maybe I could check things out when I get back and see if there's any opportunities there. We know how to cook, clean and be put in a hard day's work now. I'm sure somebody can use three or four young hardworking guys to help them out. You know I'm taking college classes in the fall. You guys may want to think about that too."

Jamal said, "If things don't work out for me, I'll definitely give you a shout."

Max agreed, "That sounds cool to me."

Sergio added, "Yeah, man! I like it."

Julius exclaimed, "Sergio, I can't believe we're talking about spending more time together after the way we first met!"

Sergio laughed, "Dude, are you ever going to get over that? I just wanted to make an impression on you."

Julius touched his temple, where there was a faint scar from his crash on the basketball court last fall. He said, "You left an impression all right! You're lucky I didn't choose to leave an impression on you. You would still be in a wheelchair."

Sergio said, "That was the old me. I'm a new creation! Right, Max?"

Max answered, "A new creation spiritually. You're still a punk in the flesh though!"

They all laughed.

It was a fun final night on the ranch for everyone, but especially for the graduating seniors. They had fun and enjoyed themselves all evening. TJ had put together a slide show from the past few years. They laughed at how much they had changed. Jamal and Katie had been there the longest and Julius the shortest amount of time. Rachel and Amber read some touching poems they had written about the kids. The four counselors brought each senior up one by one and shared good, embarrassing, and funny stories about each student. Then they spoke a blessing over each individual student. They asked for them to be blessed by God as they departed from the ranch back into the real world. Troy had a very special time of prayer for all of them. It was late when they finished the ceremony. They knew their lives had been blessed because of the Second Chance Ranch.

Chapter 31

On this beautiful Saturday morning, Victor led a caravan of cars filled with people who were going to see Julius graduate in Kingsland. Maria, Hector, and Elizabeth were all riding with him. As they drove they discussed the plans for the crisis pregnancy center.

Victor said, "Elizabeth, I have good news about the funding for the center. Pastor Patrick and I shared the vision of the center at our last meeting with area church leaders. We had three pastors who were very interested in partnering with us in creating a place for these women. Two of them have already contacted me and agreed to pledge funds for it!"

Elizabeth smiled, "That's great! I'm so excited about how God is orchestrating this ministry. I spoke with Mayor White about the old hotel downtown. He put me in contact with the owner. The cost of leasing it would be very reasonable. He said we could remodel it for the girls however we would like."

Hector said, "A building full of pregnant girls. The first thing I would do is put in sound proof walls!"

Elizabeth playfully hit Hector.

Maria said, "How exciting! God is really providing for this ministry, Elizabeth. Who do you have in mind to run it?"

Elizabeth answered, "That's one thing I'm not sure about. We need a strong female who can administer love and discipline. These girls are going to have all kinds of issues. Many will need addiction treatment and psychological care. Naturally, most will come from bad situations. I'm praying hard for God to lead the right person to us."

Victor said, "That's very wise, Elizabeth. As a church we will continue to cover this ministry in prayer."

Hector said, "God's got the perfect person who will show up at the perfect time! Hey, speaking of showing up, it looks like the church is up there on the right."

The caravan of vehicles followed Victor into the Kingsland Community Church parking lot.

Everyone made their way into the church. Victor stopped and talked to Pastor Helm in the foyer. He eventually made his way into the sanctuary where Maria had saved him a seat. There were several people there for the graduation ceremony. Julius had by far the most people there to see him. Most of the kids had immediate family or loved ones attending. Unfortunately, some of them didn't have anyone show up to watch them graduate.

The sanctuary had banners hanging on the back of the stage with the ranch's emblem and colors on them. There was one banner with the words, "Our Lord is a God of Second Chances" on it. There was a lot of greenery on the alters and stage area. Christian instrumental music played softly in the background. There were chairs on the stage facing the audience where the ranch's three board members would sit. On the other side of the stage were four chairs for the ranch counselors. They had transformed this little country church into a great place for a graduation.

As "Pomp and Circumstance" began playing, everyone stood. Two women and a man dressed in graduation gowns entered from the foyer. They walked up the center aisle and stood in front of the three chairs facing the audience. Troy, TJ, Rachel, and Amber entered next and stood in front of their chairs. Then the students who weren't graduating walked in wearing their nicer school clothes. They stood in the first two rows on the left hand side of the church. The graduating seniors finally entered in their cap and gowns and filled in the first two rows of the right side of the church.

Wanda Williams, along with everyone from Westside, was very happy to see Julius. She began to cry.

A lady from the board stepped forward and said, "Welcome to the graduation ceremony for the students of Second Chance Ranch. We are here today to recognize and honor these students who have qualified for graduation by this great state."

She stepped back to her seat.

Another board member stepped forward and said, "Please bow your head with me as we go before the Lord God in prayer."

Everyone bowed their head.

He said, "Father God, we thank you for all the blessings you have bestowed upon us. Thank you for giving us the ability to observe and to learn. You drew these students from the world and planted them here for a season. Now allow them to go back into the world healthier, because of the time they spent here. Amen."

Troy spoke and encouraged the students to be a light to the world around them. Rachel sang a solo while a video of the graduating students played. Then the students walked across the stage and received their diplomas.

At the conclusion of the ceremony the students marched outside and formed a circle. The crowd of family and friends followed them outside and gathered around their circle. The students counted down and then threw their graduation caps high into the air and cheered.

They hugged one another in celebration and then found their families and friends.

Julius found his mom and gave her a big hug. He then saw Victor and embraced him.

Julius said, "Thank you for guiding me here last fall."

Victor replied, "I'm proud of you, young man! You have done well. I'm ready to get you back home!"

Chapter 32

Julius rode home to Westside with his mom and immediately got busy figuring out where he could work. He kept in mind that his friends were considering moving there. He talked to several businesses, and although some were hiring, it just didn't feel right in his spirit. At a welcome home party, he shared his hopes of working somewhere with his friends with Victor, Reginald, and Mr. Alexander.

One afternoon a few days later, Julius got a call from Mr. Alexander. He asked Julius to come by and visit him. The two men talked for a while about how Julius was doing since he had returned home. Reginald showed up a little while later. They asked several questions about Max, Sergio, and Jamal. Julius told them he had talked to Jamal and he had gotten a job working on cars. Max and Sergio were still interested in moving to Westside.

Mr. Alexander then shocked Julius with an offer. He explained that he and Reginald had been discussing the great opportunities in the newly remodeled downtown Westside area. After hearing Julius talk about his desire to work with his friends it sounded like a perfect match. They had already made plans to lease a corner store downtown to open a new bar-b-q restaurant. The space was already being renovated. It would be ready to open for business within two weeks.

The offer was for Julius and his friends to all work there under the management of Gabriel. Mr. Alexander had worked his whole life in restaurants. He mortgaged his house and Reginald used his savings to raise the money to start the business. Gabriel had worked in a restaurant during high school. He wasn't really happy where he was working and was excited about the opportunity to manage a new restaurant. He was still in the National Guard, so he would have to plan on being gone one weekend a month and two weeks a year. He would need a strong assistant manager to cover for him when he was gone.

Julius was honored they were considering him and his friends for jobs in the business.

He asked, "What will the restaurant be named?"

Reginald answered, "Westside Bar-B-Q. What do you think?"

Julius replied, "It's simple, but okay. May I ask you something?"

Reginald said, "Of course. Julius we want your input on this. Our desire is to be relevant to your generation as well as ours."

Julius asked, "In that case, can we go look at the space?"

Mr. Alexander said, "I have the keys. Let's go."

The men rode over to the restaurant. They called Gabriel on the way and asked him to meet them there. They parked and went inside. It was obviously under construction with plastic covering the counters and painting supplies laying around. There was a large open area for dining, a counter for placing orders, and a staircase to the right. The stairs led up to a second-story balcony area that they could use for dining.

They gave Julius a tour, while explaining what would go where as they walked through the space. They entered the kitchen which had already received new stoves, smokers, and refrigerators. The kitchen area was almost finished and looked great. They moved back to the dining area.

Julius asked, "Have you thought about having live music?"

Reginald inquired, "What do you mean?"

Julius replied, "This area here could easily have a small stage where a person or small band could perform. You could watch them from the upper and lower dining areas. If we add live music on the weekends we could set ourselves apart from the competition."

Mr. Alexander agreed, "I like that idea. We could tap into a later crowd on the weekends too. That would give us an early dinner crowd and a late crowd to hear the band."

Gabriel suggested, "We could change the name to Westside Blues and Bar-B-Q!"

Julius exclaimed, "Now that's a cool name!"

Gabriel asked, "Any other ideas, Julius?"

Julius looked around, "Where are we getting our bar-b-q sauces? Are they commercial or original?"

Mr. Alexander said, "All original. I had an old family recipe for the mild and hot sauce. Gabriel came up with a spicy sauce that will knock your socks off!"

Julius asked, "Do you have plans to package the sauces where people could buy them to use at home or give as gifts?"

Gabriel said, "Reginald, I see why you were so persistent on hiring this young man. That's another great idea. We could bottle it and have it for sale."

Julius added, "We could also sell it on our website. People could literally order it from anywhere in the world. We should also come up with a cool logo and sell t-shirts."

Mr. Alexander laughingly said, "Well, Reginald, I guess Gabriel was right about having a web site. I still don't understand why we would need one for a bar-b-q joint, but I guess this generation is different."

Gabriel explained, "We'll be able to take orders online. People can see our menu and even check wait times. With the ideas Julius mentioned, we can sell our sauces and merchandise also. There's a lot of benefits to it."

Mr. Alexander said, "I know. I know. But good bar-b-q will trump a website in sales any day of the week!"

The men all laughed. This was going to be a fun adventure.

Chapter 33

The two weeks of renovation and training went by quickly. Max and Sergio moved to Westside. Wanda cleaned out a room in her house and allowed the boys to move in with her. This was only a temporary situation until they could save enough money to get a place of their own.

Julius and the guys were up early on this Friday morning. They had to get everything ready for today's grand opening. The ribbon cutting ceremony with the Chamber of Commerce was scheduled for eleven o'clock. They had to have everything ready for a big crowd.

At ten forty-five the guys had all the food prepared and the place looked fabulous. Mr. Alexander, Reginald, and Gabriel did a final walk-through and told the staff to all head outside for the ribbon cutting.

Mayor White made a short speech about the growing economy in Westside to the huge crowd. Mr. Alexander cut the big red ribbon to the cheers of everyone. The staff immediately filed back into the restaurant and got busy serving their first lunch crowd.

Everyone loved the food and the great style of the restaurant. They had cool blues music playing. It was busy until about two o'clock.

After the lunch rush they began preparing for the big opening night. They had a Christian blues singer, Sean Michel, coming in for the grand opening. Sean has a Christian ministry where he goes all around the world playing rock and blues music. He shares the love of Jesus in clubs, churches, and on street corners. They were all excited about him coming in for their opening weekend.

Victor met Hector and Ramone for lunch there. They loved the ribs. After eating, he walked through the downtown business district. Victor was amazed by all the activity going on. The buildings looked impressive with their fresh facelifts and business was booming. There were several old buildings being gutted and renovated for new stores to move into. He walked around the corner, down another block, and came to the old downtown hotel. It was in full renovation mode. Elizabeth had done a great job lining up contractors to completely overhaul the place.

Victor stopped and prayed for them to find the right person to run the crisis pregnancy center. They had interviewed two ladies, but didn't feel good about either of them. Time was getting short and they were going to need a leader in place soon.

After praying for the center, Victor turned to go back to his car, when he felt God tell him to go around the block in the other direction. At first he questioned why. Then he turned around and obeyed.

As he rounded the next corner he saw a man putting up a "Going out of Business" sign on the grocery store located on the edge of downtown. Victor felt God reveal to him this would be his new church building. Victor thought to himself, "*We're not even looking for a new church building.*"

He walked over to the man putting up the sign and said, "Hi. I'm Victor Martinez."

The man replied, "Hi, Victor. Can I help you with something?"

Victor said, "Not really. I was just noticing your sign. I'm sorry to see you're going out of business."

The man said, "Don't be! The owners of the grocery store are retiring. I own this building and the realty prices are going up around here. I'm selling it and retiring myself. It's a great day!"

Victor asked, "Do you already have a buyer?"

The man stuck out his hand and said, "I'm Dwight. No, I don't have a buyer yet. You interested?"

Victor replied, "I wasn't. But I have a feeling I might be soon."

Dwight said, "I'll be putting it up with a realtor next week. Maybe things will work out for you to buy it. What type of business are you thinking about starting?"

Victor answered, "I'm the Pastor of New Hope Church. I think God wants us to move here. I know it sounds a little crazy."

Dwight said, "Not really. I've heard about some of the things your church members are doing. You must be a bold man to inspire what I've heard about. Westside is literally changing because of the influence of you and your church."

Victor replied, "Thank you for sharing that with me. It's very encouraging to hear of the impact my congregation is having. God has been challenging us to help others as we follow Him."

Dwight said, "It's good to see a church actually making a difference in the real world. Tell you what Victor. The sooner I can sell this place, the sooner I can move to the beach. Come inside and I'll give you the lowest offer I'll take. You can think it over this weekend and let me know Monday. I'm not meeting with a realtor until then, so if we have a deal in place it would benefit both of us. I like the thought of your church moving here. It would be good for this area."

Victor replied, "Let's go look at the numbers. This may be something God wants us to do."

He followed Dwight into the store, excited to find out what God was up to.

Chapter 34

Victor was amazed at the deal Dwight was offering him. He set up an emergency meeting with New Hope Church's Board for Saturday afternoon. This was a great deal on a building and property that would be ideal for their growing church.

Everyone agreed it was a great offer, but with so many ministries already going they didn't have much money left over in the budget. They had hired Ramone and purchased a van to pick up people who needed a ride to church. They also had the recovery ministry and the Westside clean-up project they helped fund. Although their congregation continued to grow substantially, they weren't able to give enough to keep up with what they were spending.

Victor called on the board members to fervently pray and seek God's will. While it seemed like the direction God wanted them to go, Victor didn't want to make bad financial decisions and be out of God's will. If He wanted them to have this property, the Lord would make it clear.

Saturday night Victor went to Westside Blues and Bar-B-Q with Maria. They met Hector, Elizabeth, Ramone, and Mia there. They were all excited about eating some good bar-b-q together and hearing Sean Michel sing some tunes.

The place was packed. They had an hour wait for seating. Gabriel saw them in line. He walked over to them.

He said, "No need to get on the list, Pastor. I knew you would be here and I have a table reserved for you and your party."

Victor said, "Good to see you, Gabriel. Are you sure?"

Gabriel answered, "Of course. You are my honored guest. Follow me."

Everyone followed Gabriel to an eight-person table.

Maria said, "Gabriel, we only have six people."

Gabriel replied, "It's ok. You can just have a little extra room."

Victor said, "That seems wasteful with so many people waiting."

He turned to the others, "Does anyone mind if we invite a couple of people to join us?"

Hector called out, "The more the merrier!"

Everyone was fine with it.

Gabriel agreed, "I will see if anyone would like to join you!"

They began talking about how great the place looked. They all loved the ambiance. It felt like a restaurant that would be in a bigger city than Westside.

A little while later Gabriel returned with a lady who looked like she was in her late thirties.

Gabriel announced, "Pastor Victor and Maria, this young lady said she would like to join you."

She asked, "Are you sure you don't mind me joining your party?"

Maria answered, "Not at all! I'm Maria and this is my husband, Victor. That is Hector and Elizabeth. And over there is Ramone and Mia. Are you here alone?"

The lady said, "Yes, I am. I just moved to Westside yesterday and saw where they were having the grand opening here tonight. My name is Lisa."

Maria said, "It's very nice to meet you, Lisa."

Everyone welcomed Lisa into the group like they were old friends. They told her all about themselves, discussed the restaurant, and ordered their meals. Later, while they were eating, Elizabeth asked Lisa, "So what brought you to Westside?"

Lisa answered, "I'm not totally sure. I don't have any family here or a job yet. Professionally I'm a licensed therapist and counselor. I'll probably go by the hospital and see what's available. I feel like God called me here, but honestly I'm not sure exactly why. I'm just praying and seeking His will."

Maria and Elizabeth looked at one another.

Maria asked, "What type of people are you hoping to work with? Kids, adults, young, old?"

Lisa answered, "My heart is really with teenage girls who are struggling. I had some really tough times as a teen and my passion is to help young ladies through those formative years. I think in an area like this I could make a difference."

Elizabeth said, "Lisa, I would love to talk with you more about this. Would you like to be my guest at New Hope Church tomorrow morning?"

Lisa answered, "This has been a wonderful evening. I would love to visit your church tomorrow with you."

Sean Michel came up to the stage and opened up with "River Song." Everyone enjoyed the show. It had been a miraculous day.

Chapter 35

After the show ended, Gabriel, Julius, Max, and Sergio were closing up. Max took a trash bag out the back door. He walked to the dumpster and threw it in. When he turned around to go back inside, a guy was standing there with a gun pointed at him!

He froze.

The guy said, "I don't want to hurt you. I just need some money. Give me your wallet!"

As Max reached into his back pocket he said, "No problem."

He handed it to the guy. About the same time the back door opened and Julius walked out with another bag of trash.

The guy shouted, "Hold it right there!"

Julius looked at the gunman, then over at Max.

Julius said, "Just be cool man. It's all good."

The gunman commanded, "It's not all good! Give me your wallet and shut up!"

Julius gently sat the bag of trash down. He reached around into his back pocket.

The gunman said, "Slowly! Don't make any sudden moves."

Julius recognized the guy's voice. He looked intently through the darkness and asked, "Antonio, is that you?"

The gunman gasped, "Julius?"

Julius answered, "Yeah, man. It's me. I'd say it's good to see you, but I'm not a fan of having a gun pointed at me."

Antonio apologized, "Man, I'm sorry. If I would have known it was you, I wouldn't have done this. But you know how it is. Just give me your wallet and everything will be cool."

Julius said, "Antonio, you can't rob me."

Antonio said, "I don't think you understand. I AM robbing you!"

Julius explained, "No, you're not. Listen, I'm giving you all the money I have. It's a gift. Same with Max. You can have it, right Max?"

Max said, "It's a gift. Enjoy."

Gabriel had noticed the back door standing open. When he walked up to it, he heard the guys talking and realized what was happening. He went out the front and saw a patrol car down the block. He rushed over and told the policeman what was happening. The policeman called for back-up and moved toward the alley.

Back in the alley, Antonio asked, "What do you mean you're giving me the money?"

Julius said, "That's right. I won't hunt you down to get even. Here's my money. Go in peace. God loves you and I will be praying for you."

Antonio said, "I heard you got religion, but I didn't believe it 'til now. I'm sorry, Julius. I always looked up to you."

Julius said, "We're still friends, bro. You come to me when you need something. This life only ends bad for you. Trust me, I know."

Antonio slowly walked backwards down the alley. As he got to the corner, he lowered his gun and spun around to run. He was immediately knocked unconscious by a nightstick!

Chapter 36

The police arrested Antonio at the scene of the crime. Julius told him he would help him get a good lawyer. He called Victor who in turn contacted Kevin Cathey.

Kevin told Antonio he would represent him and not to say anything to anyone about the case. The earliest they could possibly get him out on bail would be on Monday. Antonio was only sixteen, but he was being held in the Westside adult jail for the time being. Kevin told him he would come by and get his side of the story.

The Westside Blues and Bar-B-Q restaurant was closed on Sundays. They had also decided to donate the first ten percent of their profits to charities, including New Hope Church. They felt they should give the first fruits of their business to God. The restaurant's grand opening weekend had gone better than any of them had dreamed. Everyone loved the food and the entertainment.

Victor preached the first service on Sunday to an almost full house. The worship was powerful and the Holy Spirit was moving. Several people came forward to pray during the invitation.

The second service was almost as full. Victor knew his church needed more space, but he had no idea how God was going to provide. He just prayed for the Lord to increase his faith. God had already sent a potential leader for the crisis pregnancy center from out of the blue. God had also protected Julius and Max from a gunman. He could certainly provide the needed space for his church's ministry.

Last summer when they needed a new building, God used Pastor Patrick and Big Oak Christian Church to provide it. Victor reminded himself his walk with Christ is by faith not by sight. He preached the second service in English and the same anointing of the Holy Spirit showed up just as powerfully. It was a refreshing time for Victor.

He and Maria went home with the twins after the services. They had just finished eating when Victor got a call.

He answered, "Hello."

The caller said, "Hello. This is Dwight. I was calling for Pastor Victor."

Victor said, "Hey, Dwight! What can I do for you?"

Dwight explained, "Victor, I received another call about the building this morning. I told them you were considering the offer we talked about yesterday, and I wouldn't discuss any other offers until you decided what you were going to do. I just wanted to keep you informed on what was happening."

Victor said, "I appreciate it. I met with our church board yesterday. We're looking at the finances. Thank you for allowing us to look into it before you entertain any other offers."

Dwight said, "We shook hands on it and I'll honor our timetable. I hope you can come up with the money. I would really feel good about selling it to your church."

Victor said, "Thank you, Dwight. I'll let you know tomorrow by noon."

As the men ended the call, Victor prayed for God to answer his prayer for the property. He felt an overwhelming sense in his spirit that this property was where God wanted to establish New Hope Church.

Victor and Maria loaded up the twins for the Sunday night gathering at New Hope Church. Sunday nights were always a fantastic night of praise and worship. As the praise band played, Victor felt confident God would provide for the church's needs.

He stepped in front of his church and explained the 3t Challenge. It was a challenge he issued regularly to his congregation and had accepted himself. He explained how we are to give God our time, our talents, and our treasures. He then asked if anyone had a testimony to share.

One after another, people stepped up and talked about the faithfulness of Jesus. Many people had sacrificed and been blessed.

A lady had begun a ministry helping people develop a budget and get their finances in order. She was an accountant, so she was very good with budgeting money. Many people didn't realize how important it was to pay attention to their finances. They worked hard for their money, but didn't have as much to show for it as they could have. She blessed many people through this ministry.

Two girls stood up together and shared how they had started praying during lunch together at the middle school. Some kids had made fun of them, but others had joined in praying with them. The girls said they didn't feel like they had any talents. During a youth lesson they had heard praying was a talent everyone could use, so they decided to just start praying. There were over thirty kids now praying at the middle school during lunch.

A girl in her twenties stepped up and told everyone how she and her husband were barely making it financially. She said they had decided to give five dollars a week to the Lord. This past week her husband had found a better job making more money.

Victor was inspired to put his faith even more in God. He hoped for a miracle to get the finances for the property by noon tomorrow.

Chapter 37

On Monday morning, Victor called Pastor Patrick Spakes and discussed the church property. They didn't see any way they could secure the deal, unless something miraculous happened before the deadline that day. After spending some time in prayer together, they each agreed to contact some of the churches in the capital city to see if they might have any ideas.

Victor made several calls. Then he prayed some more. He overwhelmingly felt like God wanted him to move New Hope Church to this location. Three minutes before twelve his phone rang!

He quickly answered it, "This is Pastor Victor. May I help you?"

His hopes were crushed when they said, "Oh, I'm sorry. I must have dialed the wrong number."

Victor asked anxiously, "Were you trying to call New Hope Church?"

The caller answered, "No. I was trying to call Lola's Taco Shack. You wouldn't happen to know their number would you?"

Victor replied flatly, "No. But they have great tacos."

The caller agreed, "Yes, they do! Thanks."

Victor hung up. He dreaded the next call he had to make. He dialed Dwight's number to inform him the church couldn't buy the property. Dwight said he was disappointed, but he would move on with the other offers.

Depressed, Victor, skipped lunch, and spent time in prayer. He questioned God on why He didn't come through. He wasn't angry at God. He just didn't understand why the Lord would lead him to this property, allow him to get a great offer, give him peace in his spirit this was the right direction for his church, and then not provide the resources. Victor prayed for wisdom and understanding.

After his time of prayer he received a call from Gabriel. He wanted to meet with Victor.

Later that afternoon Gabriel showed up at the church.

He came in and they shook hands, "Hey, Pastor. Good to see you."

Victor replied, "Good to see you too. How was business at the restaurant today?"

Gabriel answered, "It was very busy, once again. We have been astonished by the turnout. I just hope it continues."

Victor said, "With great food like you have, I'm sure it will be a success. How are Julius and the other boys working out?"

Gabriel shared, "Those guys are incredible. They have a great work ethic and are skilled in the kitchen. I hate Julius is going to have to cut back on his hours when school starts."

Victor said, "Yes, I'm proud of him for getting accepted into college. Are Max or Sergio going to take any classes this fall?"

Gabriel answered, "No. They both want to work as much as they can to build up some savings. All of them are very good with their money. I think they learned a lot about finances at Second Chance Ranch."

Victor said, "Good. Hopefully they can figure out what God wants for their lives and pursue it. So, Gabriel, what is on your mind today?"

Gabriel said, "First, I want to thank you again for all of your help. I'm healthy today, because you helped me. Now I feel like I need to help others. I've been in contact with some guys from my unit who are struggling like I was. Some are getting help, but most are too proud or embarrassed to accept any help. They are where I was or worse. I found out just this morning, a guy who was with our unit for a few weeks in Afghanistan committed suicide last night. Broke my heart. He was two years younger than me. I know I've got to do something to help."

Victor said, "I'm so sorry. That's horrible. So, how do we help?"

Gabriel answered, "I was talking with Jason Spivey. He's a military counselor at the VA. I've met with him several times. He said he would be willing to come speak if we hosted a dinner. I'm thinking we can have it here at the church and the restaurant can cater it."

Victor said, "I love the idea! We could honor all the vets and active members of the military. Let's set it up!"

Gabriel said, "Great! I was hoping you would say that. When do you think we should try to do it?"

Victor thought for a minute. He looked at his calendar, "The Fourth of July is next Monday. Do you want to try to get it together in a week? Or would you prefer to wait until Veteran's Day in November?"

Gabriel said, "I say the sooner the better. We'll advertise the event all over the area and I'll contact the guys in my unit."

Victor said, "I know you're going to busy at the restaurant and setting this up. Our church will support you with this event. It's going to be great!"

Gabriel said, "Thanks. Speaking of the restaurant, I better get back over there to get ready for tonight. I'll be planning and praying!"

Chapter 38

The next week was a whirlwind of activity for Victor and Gabriel. Victor already had all of his normal church duties to perform. In addition to those, New Hope Church was sponsoring a Fourth of July performance in Redemption Park. They were calling it "Pops and Praise." The Hurst's were putting together a whole music set incorporating both praise and patriotic songs. They would perform before and during the fireworks. The local Veterans of Foreign Wars organization sponsored the fireworks show each year.

Gabriel was busy with the restaurant. He had booked another blues band for Friday and Saturday night. He contacted Jason Spivey and got him to commit to speak at the dinner the next Monday night before the fireworks show. He also contacted local TV, radio, and newspapers to announce the event. He had decided to call the dinner for the servicemen the "Westside Warriors Appreciation Banquet."

On Saturday night Victor, Maria, Hector, and Elizabeth went to eat at Westside Blues and Bar-B-Q. They had Theresa and her friend babysit for them.

Even as busy as Victor was, he knew he needed to make time to take Maria on a date. His mentor, Pastor Patrick, had stressed to him how important it was to stay connected to his wife and family, even during hectic times.

After he ate, Gabriel took him back to the restaurant's office. They spent about ten minutes confirming all their plans and had a quick prayer.

Victor made it back to their table as the band began to play. They had a good time listening to the blues band. The restaurant was once again overflowing with people.

On Sunday morning, New Hope Church was full. Victor thought about the building downtown he had wanted and how his church could use the added space. He shoved the thought away and focused on sharing the love of God with everyone this July 3rd morning.

His sermon was titled, "The Gift of Freedom."

After an awesome time of prayer and Spirit-filled worship in song, Victor stood to preach. He shared how America was settled by those seeking religious freedom. God was undeniably worshiped by most of our founding fathers. Victor shared how George Washington returned from battles with holes in his jacket from musket balls, but miraculously wasn't hurt. He taught how we aren't a theocracy, but that a Judeo-Christian heritage was what our laws and Constitution were founded upon.

Victor explained how the Civil War brought a new challenge for this great nation, but out of that horrible conflict came more freedom for all. Over and over the Lord has blessed this nation to be a light to the world.

He explained how it's hard to imagine what our nation would be if the Lord removed his blessing from us.

Victor shared how Westside was a great example of what happens to a city who obeys God. As following God was abandoned over the past few decades, Westside went downhill. Families were fractured, poverty was common, and crime was rampant. In the past year, as people have begun to give of themselves and obey God's word, those trends are reversing.

Victor ended by sharing how freedom is never free. For our country, freedom was bought with the blood and sacrifice of heroic soldiers. For our souls, freedom was paid for through the blood and sacrifice of Jesus.

Many people responded to the alter call.

Chapter 39

After the first service, once several people had left, Julius caught up with Victor.

He said, "Hey, Pastor Vic. Have you got a minute?"

Victor answered, "Sure, Julius. How are things at the restaurant?"

Julius said, "Really good. We've been super busy and I couldn't ask for a better boss. Gabriel is great."

Victor replied, "That's very good to hear. I spoke with Kevin Cathey about Antonio. He said bail was still denied, but he's working on a plea deal to get him to the Second Chance Ranch. I spoke with Troy on his behalf and they are down to two open spots left. We should know more before too long."

Julius said, "Thank you for helping him out. He's a good kid at heart. Troy could really help him a lot."

Victor agreed, "Yes, I believe you're right. He certainly helped you. Julius, you have totally forgiven Antonio for robbing you at gunpoint. I know we spoke last week about it, but it's really something."

Julius said, "I know we talked about the robbery last week, but actually I have been dealing with some other stuff that happened that night. I wanted to talk to you about it."

Victor asked, "What's on your mind?"

Julius shared, "Troy taught me to process things, but to share them once I have. When Antonio had that gun pointed at me, all I could think about was wanting to see my dad. I wasn't sure until that very moment I even wanted to meet him. My mom told me he's in prison. I'm don't know if he would see me if I visited."

Victor thought for a moment, "If you want to meet him, maybe it would be wise to write him first. You can tell him about yourself, and give him a chance to wrap his mind around meeting you. It might be better than just showing up unexpectedly and surprising him."

Julius agreed, "That's probably a smart way to go about it. I'm scared to contact him, but I know it's what I need to do."

Victor said, "We'll pray about it and I'll be happy to help you write your letter. I'm proud of you pursuing this. I know it's not easy."

Julius said, "Thank you, Pastor Vic."

The guys shook hands and Julius went to get a seat. Victor ran into Elizabeth and Hector coming in for the second service with Pedro and Pablo.

He called out, "Good morning!"

Hector answered, "Good morning, Victor!"

Pedro walked over to Victor and gave him a high-five.

Victor asked, "Are you excited about children's church this morning?"

Pedro nodded his head.

Elizabeth, handing Pablo to Hector said, "Please take the boys to their classes, Hector. I need to talk to Victor about the crisis pregnancy."

Hector laughed, "Are you having a crisis pregnancy? Shouldn't you be talking to me about it?"

Elizabeth exclaimed, "Not me! You know I'm talking about the center. Although, if I was pregnant again already it would be a crisis! Take your boys, Mister!"

Hector replied, "Sure. Give me that sweet little boy. Come on, Pedro. Let's get you to class. See you in service, Victor."

Victor said, "Sounds good, Cuz. Have fun, Pedro!"

Pedro waved back to him.

Victor asked Elizabeth, "So how are things going with the center? I went by there and saw they were working hard on getting it ready."

She answered, "It's going great! With the financial commitments, we should be able to get the hotel renovated and be up and running this fall. I've been talking to Lisa and I really believe God brought her here to Westside to run this ministry."

Victor said, "I saw her in church last week sitting with you. So she meets our requirements for the position?"

Elizabeth said, "She exceeds our requirements. Lisa got pregnant when she was sixteen. She finished high school, then joined the National Guard and went to college. Her daughter is now in her senior year of college. Lisa has never married. She loves the idea of being a house mom for these girls. She understands they will need love and discipline. I think we need to move forward by having the board interview her and getting her approved. It's like God brought her here at the perfect time."

Victor said, "It sounds like He did! He certainly has a way of showing up right on time."

Chapter 40

On Monday morning Victor and Maria got ready for the big Fourth of July celebration. They spent the day together with the kids. About four o'clock in the afternoon Victor arrived at the church. Gabriel and the team he had assembled were finishing up the decorations and beginning to prepare dinner.

As Victor pulled up to the church he saw a big red, white, and blue banner that said "Westside Warriors Appreciation Banquet." He admired the small American flags lining the walkway as he walked up the sidewalk to the church. He entered the building and saw there was a table for greeters to register people and get them seated. There were enough tables and chairs to seat one hundred fifty people. The tables had white tablecloths and decorative "Thank You" signs all over them.

The delicious smell of bar-b-q filled the room. He looked up at the stage where there was a flag from each branch of the military. Along one wall was a booth promoting the VFW and another for the Wounded Warrior Project. There were also several tables and shelves filled with old and new military pictures.

He made his way back to the kitchen to give them a hand.

He saw Gabriel and said, "Hey! Good to see you! Everything looks wonderful!"

Gabriel replied, "Thanks! It's coming together! I think it's going to be a terrific event. I've had lots of guys tell me they're going to be here."

Victor said, "Sounds good. How can I help?"

Gabriel answered, "We're opening the doors at six. We'll begin serving dinner at six-thirty. About seven-fifteen we'll begin the videos and talks. We'll be done by eight to have plenty of time for our little surprise for them. We want to travel to Redemption Park while there's still some daylight. There's a special section of seating reserved for our group when they arrive. The fireworks show starts at nine. If you could help finish setting up the chairs that would be great!"

Victor replied, "You got it!"

At six o'clock the doors opened to a long line of servicemen. There was a mixture of active-duty and retired members. They signed in and were escorted to their seats. Some of them stood around talking to friends while others browsed through the booths and military pictures set up on some tables against the walls.

At six-thirty Gabriel stepped to the podium. He enthusiastically said, "Welcome to our first annual Westside Warriors Appreciation Banquet. Thank you for being here, and thank you for your service!"

Gabriel then said a blessing for the food and asked everyone to have a seat. They began taking their seats as the food was served. People kept coming in. The place was completely full. Victor removed the pictures from the tables along the walls to add some additional seating. Everyone loved the food and enjoyed talking, laughing, and sharing stories of their glory days.

The volunteer servers cleaned off the tables as Gabriel stood again to speak.

He said, "Tonight is all about thanking you for your service. The life of a soldier is unique. Sometimes it's you against the world and at other times it's the closest knit team of people imaginable. The bonds formed in boot camp, in training and on the battlefield are some of the strongest bonds people can achieve. As your brother-in-arms, I salute you, my brothers and sisters!"

Everyone stood and saluted back to Gabriel.

Then he led them in the Pledge of Allegiance.

He said, "I pledge allegiance to the flag of the United States of America, and to the republic for which it stands, one nation under God, indivisible, with liberty and justice for all."

Gabriel continued, "You may be seated. We'll now have a video followed by a message from Colonel Jason Spivey."

The lights went down and a video began playing, starting with paintings of scenes from the Revolutionary War and going through all of America's wars. Pictures of soldiers laughing, fighting and celebrating were all displayed. It was a stirring presentation of soldier's heroism and sacrifice. The video culminated with a quote from George Washington, the Father of the United States of America, saying, "While we are zealously performing the duties of good citizens and soldiers, we certainly ought not to be inattentive to the higher duties of religion. To the distinguished character of Patriot, it should be our highest glory to add the more distinguished character of Christian."

The lights came up as Colonel Spivey moved to the podium to speak.

He began, "It is an honor to stand before so many hero's on this very special day in our history. You are the men and women who have sacrificed for the continued freedom we enjoy as a nation. I am one of you. I served in battle during Operation Desert Storm. Of all the honors I received the Purple Heart is my most precious. I left my right leg in a field hospital somewhere on the other side of the world. Learning to walk again wasn't the only struggle I had when I returned home.

"I experienced war. It's crazy and chaotic. Sometimes being wounded ourselves isn't as hard as losing some of our brothers and sisters in battle. Mentally trying to understand what you experienced is sometimes just as hard as healing from the physical injuries.

"I struggled when I came home. It didn't feel right. Finally, I came around to admitting I needed help dealing with the mental, as well as physical, wounds. I got counseling and dealt with my issues.

"Afterward I decided I wanted to help others who had struggles. I got my master's degree in psychiatry and joined the Veteran's Administration. Helping fellow soldier's deal with the transition from combat to civilian life is my passion. If you would like to talk with me about anything, my number is in the pamphlet you received when you arrived.

"Thank you for your service! May God bless you and may God bless America!"

The assembly erupted in applause.

Gabriel came back to the podium and said, "Thank you Colonel Spivey. I personally have been helped by this great man. He's someone who genuinely cares about our military service members.

"We have a very special surprise for you now. I need for you to exit in single file out to the parking lot. You will get instructions on what to do once you're out there."

The assembly was curious about what was planned outside. They exited the church in an orderly manner. As they exited, they were greeted by clapping people lining the church sidewalk on both sides. They walked through the cheers and applause to the parking lot where there was a line of vehicles with trailers behind them. The soldiers, young and old, climbed aboard the trailers. Once everyone was loaded they began a parade through Westside.

Somehow in one week, Victor and Gabriel had not only organized a great banquet, but a surprise parade as well.

Chapter 41

As the parade made its way through downtown Westside, people lined the sidewalks. The trailers had candy provided for the soldiers to throw. The crowds of people walking to the fireworks show stopped to enjoy the parade. Store owners had put up signs thanking them for their service.

The parade arrived at the entrance of Redemption Park. The swarm of military veterans and active-duty members moved to the sectioned-off seating area for them over by the lake.

The Hurst's from New Hope Church led a band in playing a mixture of praise and patriotic music. At nine o'clock the first firework exploded into the dark sky. The band continued to play as the fireworks lit up the darkness.

Victor found Maria and the twins. They were sitting with several members from New Hope Church. Everyone was enjoying the festivities.

Victor said, "Hey Maria! Great fireworks show, isn't it?"

She answered, "Yes it is! How did everything go at the banquet?"

As fireworks exploded overhead he answered, "Better than I ever could have imagined! Wow! That was a pretty one! Looks like Daniela is enjoying the show!"

Maria smiled, "Yes, she is. Gabriela on the other hand is somehow sleeping through all of this excitement."

Victor looked over at the stroller holding his sleeping baby girl and smiled. He took Daniela from Maria as more colors filled the sky.

The show lasted about thirty minutes. Everyone applauded as the thunderous explosions stopped and quietness filled the air.

As they made their way out of the park, several people thanked Victor for all he and his church were doing.

Victor saw Reginald, "Hi! Good to see you, brother."

He replied, "Hey, Victor. Maria. Really good fireworks show tonight. I loved the music."

Victor said, "They did a wonderful job. It added a lot to the beautiful fireworks display. You look tired, Reginald. Long day?"

He replied, "Long night last night. I had to go stay with a young man who was struggling through major withdrawals. It wore me out. But we survived and God has given me strength to make it through today."

Maria said, "You go home and get some rest. You've earned it."

Reginald said, "Thanks. Doing God's work is worth it, but it's not easy. Have a good night."

They said their goodbyes and walked toward the car.

Victor saw Mayor White, "Good evening, Mayor."

Mayor White greeted them, "Hello, Victor and Maria. What a wonderful night in Westside!"

Victor replied, "Yes it is, Mayor."

He said, "Victor, you should be proud. Tonight would not have been a tenth of the event it was without your influence on our town. Maria, you have a first-class husband. And you know what they say: behind every good husband is a great wife!"

Maria said, "Be careful, Mayor. You're starting to sound like a politician."

They all laughed.

He said, "Seriously, you have both benefitted our community far more than you know. Did you hear the grocery store on the end of town has sold? At least Dwight told me he had an offer he was planning on accepting. It will be another new business in town."

Victor's heart sank. He hadn't shared with Mayor White that he had pursued the building. He was still hoping for a miracle. God had not given him any peace about losing the property.

He asked, "Who's buying it?"

Mayor White answered, "That's the part I'm not overly excited about. A company who specializes in nightclubs bought it. They are going to renovate it into a large dance club."

Victor exclaimed, "A nightclub? That's just what our community doesn't need!"

Mayor White said, "I understand and while I agree with you, they have the right to exist just as much as anyone. There will be rules they must abide by. I knew you wouldn't be happy about it. That's why I wanted to tell you myself."

Victor calmed down a bit, "Thank you for telling me personally. We're fighting addictions and depravity constantly in our town. I just hate to see another place open where I know people will struggle with staying clean."

Mayor White encouraged him, "I understand. Keep fighting the good fight, Victor. You are making a difference."

Victor said, "Thanks. I'm not giving up on that property yet."

Mayor White said, "Good! Personally, I'd rather see a more positive family friendly business in the space. Either way, I'll support whatever establishment moves in there. As long as they obey all the laws."

Victor said, "I understand. Thank you."

Chapter 42

Later that week, Julius stopped by to talk to Victor. He saw him and said, "Hey, Pastor Vic."

Victor replied, "Hey, Julius. Good to see you. How was work?"

Julius answered, "Going great! Lunch was busy again. We're still constantly slammed."

Victor said, "That's good to hear. Gabriel said you, Max, and Sergio are doing a fantastic job. He's very impressed with the work ethic you guys have."

Julius explained, "It's a fun place to work. And a lot easier than working on the ranch!"

Victor laughed and then asked, "So Julius, what did you want to talk about?"

Julius replied, "I've written a letter to my dad. I wanted you to read it and let me know what you think."

Victor said, "I'd be happy to. Do you have it with you?"

Julius answered, "Yes sir. I have it right here." He pulled an envelope from his back pocket and handed it to Victor.

Victor opened it and read it quietly to himself.

"Dear Cecil,

I recently found out you knew Wanda Williams many years ago. She is my mother. She revealed to me, not too long ago, you are my father. I don't expect anything from you. From what I understand, you will not be getting out of prison anytime soon. I think it is normal for a boy to want to meet his father. If you are willing to meet with me, I will come visit you. If you would rather not meet me, I will honor your wishes. My mom said she believes there was a time when you cared about her. Please let me know what you would like me to do.

Julius Williams

Victor said, "I think it's a very good letter, Julius. You shared your feelings and showed respect for his. Are you ready to mail it?"

He answered, "Yes, sir. I am."

Victor said, "All right. I'll put it in the outgoing mail for you."

Julius said, "Thank you. Could we pray over it first?"

Victor answered, "I think that's a very good idea."

The two men kneeled down and prayed for God's will to be done in this situation. Just as they had finished praying, Kevin Cathey walked into the church.

He announced, "Hey guys! I've got good news!"

Victor asked, "What's up, Kevin?"

He answered, "I just got out of a meeting with the prosecutor in Antonio's case. They are going to allow him to go to Second Chance Ranch! It's really unusual for them to agree to this if a gun is involved in the crime. Julius, since you were the victim, your testimony went a long way in helping them decide to let him go there."

Julius exclaimed, "That's awesome! Troy and TJ are going to help him a lot! When is he going to be leaving?"

Kevin said, "Tomorrow morning. The judge should sign off on it in about an hour. He's a very fortunate young man. They were leaning toward prosecuting him as an adult. This is a blessing."

Victor asked, "Could we go see him off in the morning?"

Kevin answered, "I'll meet you at the bus station at eight!"

The next morning Victor, Julius, and Kevin were waiting for Antonio at the bus station.

Victor asked, "Does this remind you of anything, Kevin?"

He answered, "Yes it does, Pastor. About a year ago we were right here waiting on another young man to go find his way to the Second Chance Ranch."

Julius said, "I can't believe it was a year ago. In some ways it seems like a long time ago, and in other ways it seems like just yesterday. I'm just glad the ranch was there for me, and I'm glad it's still there for Antonio."

Kevin observed, "This is a much better situation for him. He will have a great opportunity to overcome his issues."

Victor said, "You know, Kevin, it was right here where you first shared with me, your desire to help people who needed good legal representation and couldn't afford it. I would say it's been an overwhelming success."

Kevin replied, "Well, the 3t Challenge you issued led me to that decision. It has been so rewarding to help the less fortunate."

Victor said, "You've made a big difference in several people's lives."

Kevin replied, “We’ve helped in nineteen different cases, including Antonio’s. It has been very rewarding.”

Julius said, "I really appreciate you helping him. Look, there's Antonio and his mom now."

Antonio walked over to the group of guys as his mom followed him.

He said, "Thank you for helping me avoid prison. Julius, I'm sorry for what I did."

Julius asked, "Can Antonio and I have a minute?"

Antonio's mom agreed and the guys stepped a few feet away.

Julius asked, "Are you ready for this, Antonio?"

Antonio answered, "I guess so. It's better than going to prison. Like you said, maybe God is going to use this to help me."

Julius said, "I'm glad to hear that, Antonio. Troy Speer, the ranch director will meet you at the bus station. He'll be the bald headed guy wearing the Second Chance Ranch t-shirt. I messaged him last night. He's a strong Christian man. Do your best to learn all you can from him."

Antonio said, "I will, Julius."

Julius continued, "I'll check in on your family and make sure they're all right. You concentrate on becoming the man God wants you to be!"

Antonio said, "Thanks, man."

The terminal's loudspeaker announced the bus for Kingsland was now loading.

Antonio's mom stepped over and took his hand. He shook hands with Kevin and Victor, then walked with his mom over to the loading area.

Julius silently prayed for Antonio, and also thanked God for seeing him through his journey to the ranch and back.

Chapter 43

The crisis pregnancy center was finally ready for its grand opening on this August day. This would be one of the few times the public would be able to visit beyond the foyer area. There were politicians, including the governor, from all over the state here today for the ribbon cutting.

Victor was inside helping Elizabeth make sure everything was ready.

He said, "Elizabeth, the place looks great! Everyone, including the governor, will be very impressed."

She said, "Thank you. Lisa has been such a great help. So has the team from the church. I could have never done all this without them."

Victor replied, "You were the visionary who dreamed all this up. It was your idea. That's why it's called Elizabeth's House."

She replied, "I told you not to use my name! It makes me sound pretentious."

Victor laughed, "Anyone who knows you realizes you are very humble. It's a great name. Will Tamica be here today?"

Elizabeth answered, "Yes, she will! She finally got to take Shonda home. It was good of Ramone and Mia to take her in until she can find a place of her own."

Victor said, "It certainly was. They had the extra bedroom and Mia loves babies. It's still a stretch to take someone into your home. Ramone told me it was their way of following the 3t Challenge. I'm proud of them."

She replied, "I can't believe you got the governor to be here for the grand opening. That's exciting!"

He said, "Her office actually contacted us about speaking today. They said she is very impressed with the turnaround Westside is experiencing. With the growing economy, increased public services and volunteerism at a record high, Westside is a great example of what urban areas can become. We better get out there. It looks like it's time to share your house with the world!"

Elizabeth smiled. She was honored God had used her to develop a place where desperate young girls can find hope and help.

They stepped out of the front door together and took their places in the gathering crowd. The local and state-wide press were there to cover the ribbon-cutting ceremony since the governor was speaking.

The street in front of Elizabeth's House was blocked off for the event. Mayor White stepped to the small podium first. He greeted the crowd, other local leaders, and the governor. He shared some statistics on Westside's economic increases and decreasing crime rate. He then introduced Elizabeth Gonzales to share about the vision of the center.

Elizabeth told the story of almost losing her baby and how the Lord used that situation to connect her with Tamica. Through her relationship with Tamica, God led her to start Elizabeth's House. Everyone was touched by her story.

The governor was introduced as the next speaker. She stepped forward to the podium.

She began, "It's an honor to be around such a wonderful group of people. I've been hearing stories about the tremendous changes going on in Westside and the communities around our capital city. It's awesome to meet some of the people who are making these changes happen.

"As a society it is our responsibility to be good citizens. It's something special to see those of you who are not only doing your duty, but taking up the slack where others have fallen short. It's inspiring to drive through Westside and see the changes taking place.

"Unfortunately in our generation morality has sunk to a new low. Families are torn apart and children are suffering the consequences. This has resulted in decreased school graduation rates, higher rates of substance abuse and increased pregnancies in our teenagers. A place like Elizabeth's House will help these young ladies have healthier pregnancies which will result in healthier babies.

"Elizabeth's House will also help these young ladies continue their educations and learn job skills. This is not a place where girls simply come to receive a handout. It's a home where ladies can better themselves while they go through some major changes in their lives.

"On behalf of our great state, I applaud everyone who has had a hand in creating and developing Elizabeth's House."

Everyone clapped and cheered.

Victor took the microphone next.

He said, "Please bow your heads as we go to the Lord in prayer. Father we thank You for giving us the command and ability to help one another. Help us to always give thanks to You for our blessings, while simultaneously looking for ways to bless others. We ask You to bless Elizabeth's House with love and hope. Thank you for giving us the perfect example of love and hope through your Son Jesus. Amen."

Elizabeth, Mayor White, and the governor took a pair of scissors and posed for pictures behind the big red ribbon. They all cut the ribbon at the same time and everyone cheered.

The crowd filed into Elizabeth's House to see the crisis pregnancy center for themselves. It could house up to eight girls at one time. They each had their own room and would be allowed to live there until their baby was three months old.

Victor saw Julius outside in the crowd. He made his way over to him.

He said, "Hey Julius! How are you doing?"

Julius replied, "Great! I wanted to come support the House. Hey, I got a letter back from my dad! I'm so happy he wrote me back. He asked about mom and what things were like around here now. He didn't say if he wanted to meet me, but asked me to write him again."

Victor said, "That's good! I bet he'll want to meet you. It may take a little time. Be patient with him."

Julius said, "Oh, I am. I'm just happy he responded. That alone is an answer to prayer. I'm going to check this place out before I head over for my shift at the restaurant. You coming in?"

Victor answered, "Maybe in a little while. Go ahead. I'll see you soon."

Julius went in and Victor walked down the street. He went around the corner to where the old grocery store had been. There was lots of activity going on all over the property. It looked like they had finished gutting the building, and were doing some interior work. Victor silently prayed for wisdom and understanding. He felt like God was telling him, not audibly but in his spirit, to be silent.

Victor stood silently looking across the busy parking lot. He felt God tell him to walk to the corner of the property. Victor obeyed. When he got to the corner he stopped and stood silently, trying to hear his Lord. God told him to bow down and ask Him for the property. This seemed very weird to Victor. He looked around at the traffic passing by. He questioned what he was hearing, but couldn't deny he felt it was God's instruction. Victor humbled himself, bowed down, and asked God for the property for New Hope Church.

After praying Victor stood back up. Although this was way out of his comfort zone, he felt like he had been obedient to the Lord. Victor quieted his spirit once again. God led him to the next corner of the large property. Once again, God told him to kneel down and ask Him for the property. Victor obeyed immediately this time.

This happened until he had been to all four corners of the property. Then he felt God tell him to go in peace. Victor walked back to his car wondering whether he had just done the craziest thing or the boldest thing in his walk with Jesus. But in his spirit he felt overwhelming peace.

Chapter 44

The next morning at seven a.m. Victor's phone rang.

He answered it, "Hello."

He heard, "Victor! This is Dwight. Things are falling apart on the deal with my building you wanted. The company hit some hard times losing a lawsuit in another city. They were hit with serving alcohol to underage kids and some employees were dealing drugs out of the nightclub. They had a ninety-day back out agreement, although I get to keep their down payment. They're pulling out and taking their losses. I thought I'd give you another shot at it. Are you interested?"

Victor's head was spinning. He couldn't believe what he was hearing.

He asked, "Is it the same amount we discussed earlier?"

Dwight answered, "Yes. But it's a better deal for you now. The down payment has already been made. The thousands you would have spent on gutting it has already been done. They have also rewired the building bringing it up to code. Getting it now is a much better deal than it would have been when you originally were looking at it."

Victor said, "It sounds like it. We are in slightly better shape financially, but still a long way from being able to finance it. Can you give me a day or two to pray about it and research our options?"

Dwight answered, "Sure. I really would like your church to have this property. Let me know something as soon as you can."

Victor hung up and prayed, "Lord, You know I'm happy with New Hope Church staying in our current location and serving you right there. This new property wasn't my idea, it was Yours. I'm doing my best to listen to You and to be obedient. You keep bringing this before me. I only want Your will for New Hope Church. If we are supposed to relocate, it is in Your hands. I know it's only through Your power we could think about doing something this bold. I put my trust in You. Amen"

Victor's phone immediately began ringing.

He answered it, "Hello."

A man on the other end said, "I'm calling for Pastor Victor Martinez."

Victor said, "This is Victor. How may I help you?"

He replied, "Hi, Pastor. My name is Shawn Wood. I live in the capital city and attend church downtown there. We had a visitor come and speak about three months ago. He was the pastor of Big Oak Christian Church. His name was Patrick Spakes."

Victor said, "I know Pastor Patrick very well. He is a good friend of mine."

Shawn continued, "He issued something he called the 3t Challenge to our church. He shared how the Bible teaches we should follow God by giving Him our first fruits. I accepted the 3t Challenge and began looking for ways to give God my time, talents, and treasures. A few weeks later our pastor mentioned praying for New Hope Church in Westside. God has blessed me with a great career and I'm financially comfortable. I felt an overwhelming urge God wanted me to give your church a large sum of money. But I was disobedient."

Victor could hear the despair and brokenness in Shawn's voice.

Victor said, "None of us walk perfectly with the Lord."

Shawn answered, "Thank you. I appreciate your kindness. I have had the most miserable past two months of my life. My disobedience to God has broken me. I know without a doubt I'm supposed to give you this gift or live in regret. Please forgive me for my lack of obedience."

Victor answered, "Brother, you have my complete and total forgiveness. I'm sorry you have had to walk this difficult road, but I'm proud of your obedience today."

Shawn said, "Thank you, Pastor. Would it be possible for me to meet you at your church this morning? I can't wait to get this check out of my hands and into yours!"

Victor answered, "I'll meet you at New Hope Church in an hour. Would you mind if I ask what amount God has laid upon your heart to give?"

Shawn told him the amount. Victor was surprised by the large amount.

Victor asked, "Shawn, are you sure you want to donate this much money?"

Shawn answered, "You don't understand. I cannot wait to donate it, Pastor. I'll meet you in an hour!"

Victor hung up the phone and smiled. The amount was exactly what New Hope Church needed to acquire the new property and stay within their budget.

As Victor drove over to the church he thought about the events over the past few months. He remembered how God had led him to the grocery store and meeting Dwight. Victor wondered why God had allowed all the events to unfold the way they did. Was it to build his faith? Shawn Wood's faith? Was it to teach him to listen to God and humble himself like he did yesterday? Victor wondered what might have happened if Shawn hadn't been obedient today. Would God have provided in a different way? What if he hadn't been obedient yesterday to kneel and pray in public? He thought about the Bible verse in Isaiah 55:8 where God says, "For My thoughts are not your thoughts, nor are your ways My ways," declares the Lord.

Victor thought to himself, *"God is teaching me that while I might not always understand how He is working, I can still always trust Him."*

Chapter 45

Two weeks later New Hope Church had secured Dwight's property and were making plans for the building and grounds. It was going to allow them much more space for ministering to the Westside community. They were also able to keep the other location by the school for the after-school program. God had provided abundantly.

Victor was eating lunch with Julius today. They were sitting at a table eating ribs.

Julius said, "Pastor Vic, I always hear how people get tired of eating the food where they work."

Victor asked, "Are you tired of the food here?"

Julius answered, "Not at all! I love this food. I don't think I could get tired of it."

Victor said, "It is delicious. Are you ready to start classes on Monday?"

Julius answered, "Yes, sir! I'm taking sixteen hours. With the nine I already have, I'll almost be a sophomore by Christmas. How cool is that?"

Victor replied, "Pretty cool. Do you have everything you need?"

He said, "I'm all set! Can't wait to start school again."

Victor said, "Good deal. We have a special guest visiting New Hope this Sunday."

Julius asked, "Oh really. Who is it?"

Victor answered, "Jamie Spakes. You remember I told you about her writing the devotional using Daniel's journal. Well, it got published and she's going to come share about it with us. She'll be a junior at Lost Creek High School this fall."

He said, "Awesome. It will be good to see her again. I know Theresa will be excited."

Victor said, "Yes. She has been asking me about it for weeks. Have you heard anything more from your dad?"

He answered, "Yes, sir. We have written back and forth several times now. He still hasn't mentioned meeting me yet. I think it will happen though. At least I hope it does."

Victor said, "Hang in there, Julius. It's all in God's hands and in His timing. Just keep praying and trusting Him."

He said, "I'm praying every day. I better get back to work. My lunch break is almost over."

Victor said, "It was good to visit with you. I'm proud of you!"

Julius smiled and went back to the kitchen.

Gabriel came by Victor's table.

He asked, "Was everything good today, Pastor?"

Victor replied, "No, Gabriel, it was great! I'm glad things have worked out so well here. The boys have good jobs, the restaurant is a success, and you seem really happy managing it."

He said, "It has been a blessing. Julius had a great idea buying the sandwich cart to take out to Redemption Park during lunches. It has increased our sales a lot. We've had to hire a couple of more employees to keep up. Julius could manage a restaurant himself. He's a natural. I'm going to miss him working here during the week."

Victor said, "Yes. He'll still be here on the weekends, right?"

Gabriel said, "Most definitely. You know Max brought up an interesting idea the other day. He mentioned opening another location or two. One downtown in the capital city and possibly one over in Lost Creek. We'll have to look at the costs and pray about it first."

Victor asked, "Who is going to replace Julius during the week?"

He answered, "I have a couple of military buddies who have shown some interest. One of them is Ricky who has been visiting church with me."

Victor replied, "You're going to have to narrow it down. Ever since our Fourth of July event you have brought lots of friends to church."

He smiled, "I'm so glad we were able to have it. Colonel Spivey helped several people who needed it. Some of the younger folks connected with older vets who they met there and have helped them through some struggles. God truly blessed that event."

Victor said, "I'm proud of the man you have become, Gabriel. You are a good father, husband, and friend."

He said, "Thank you, Pastor. That means a lot coming from you. How is everything shaping up on the new church campus?"

Victor replied, "Very good. We're going to really be able to help a lot more people with this new facility. I'm excited about the potential we have to invest in the people of Westside. If things go well we should be able to have our first service there Christmas Sunday!"

Gabriel said, "That would be amazing! It's exciting to see all the changes that are taking place around here."

Victor agreed, "Yes it is, Gabriel. More exciting than the new buildings and stores is the new attitude the people have. I see more hope in our people, and I see God changing lives. It's great to be part of this physical and spiritual renewal. I pray God continues to bless us with His love."

Chapter 46

On Sunday morning New Hope Church was preparing for another capacity crowd. JJ Smith and Jamie Spakes made their way inside to the front where the worship band was talking. Theresa saw her good friend and ran to hug her.

JJ said, "Uh, I'm here too, Theresa."

She laughed, "JJ, you're a mess. Give me a hug."

Dwayne made his way over to his friends. He hugged them, "It's great to see both of you! How's it going?"

JJ replied, "College is tough, but I'm making it. Jamie keeps me in line and makes me study."

Jamie added, "We're doing great. It's so good to see everyone. I hear you're getting a new larger building. How exciting!"

Dwayne said, "Yes, we are. We're gonna have some cool new toys for the worship band."

JJ said, "Maybe I could join in with the band today. I play a mean pair of spoons!"

Everyone laughed.

Victor came up to the group.

He greeted them, "Jamie! JJ! It's good to see you both. I'm excited to hear about your devotional this morning, Jamie."

Jamie replied, "It's awesome to be here. Thank you so much for having us."

Victor said, "It's our privilege. You'll be speaking through an interpreter in our first service. Just take your time and you'll do fine. I'll call you up after our worship in song, before I preach this morning. Sound good?"

Jamie said, "Yes sir! I'm excited to worship with all of you today."

Victor said, "We're happy you are here. Everyone grab hands and let me pray for our service this morning."

They all took joined hands in a circle and prayed for God to be with them. They asked Him to meet each person's needs. They prayed for the Holy Spirit to convict people of their sin and for them to receive God's free gift of forgiveness and Salvation.

After the prayer time, the service began. Victor welcomed everyone and the band led them into a time of praise and worship. After the worship set, Victor introduced Jamie Spakes.

She came forward, "It is such a blessing to worship with all of you this morning. This is the first time I've spoken through an interpreter. My Spanish is very limited. I mostly know Mexican restaurant menu items."

Everyone laughed.

"It was about a year and a half ago when I met many of you for the first time. I was here with my family and members of Big Oak Christian Church getting this building ready for services. Theresa and I met while painting the flowery mural out front. Your church has been such a blessing to me and my family.

"Just over one year ago my dad was preaching a revival here. Julius Williams, along with many others, got saved that week. As many of you know my brother, Daniel, was a big part of the revival. He helped with the games, played with the kids, and played the drums out at Redemption Park on the final night. On his way home, Daniel hit a deer and swerved into a tree. He was instantly killed in the wreck.

"I fell apart for a while after Daniel died. I loved him so much. Just after he died, I found his journal. It's hard for a sister to say this about her brother, but he wasn't completely dumb."

Everyone laughed again.

Jamie continued, "I took his journal entries and combined them with scripture and quotes to create a daily devotional. I believe Daniel would be proud to be inspiring people with his thoughts."

Jamie paused for a moment and then continued, "JJ, who is here with me this morning, was in the wreck with Daniel. We stopped on the drive over here and saw the tree they hit that night. It was tough to be in the spot where my brother lost his life. If Daniel were here today, I believe he would tell you to enjoy life to the fullest. And you can only do that by following Jesus. He's the ultimate hope for us all; in this life and the next.

"I'm going to share today's devotional to give you an idea of what each day's study is like. The top of the page reads: I Corinthians 15:33: Do not be deceived: 'Bad company corrupts good morals.'

"Daniel Spakes' journal entry: I've been struggling with some of my friendships. I want to be careful not to judge anyone, but I realize the Bible teaches me to be careful about who I hang out with. I have realized I act a lot like the people I'm around. If I want to become more like Jesus, I need to spend time with people who have the same goal. I think I should still hang out with people who are different than me, but my closest friends and the majority of my time should be spent with people I want to be like. My dad says, 'If you lay down with dogs, don't be surprised when you get up with fleas.' That's kind of corny, but it does make sense. If I hang around people who tell dirty jokes, brag about sinning, or bully other kids, I'm more likely to be okay with those things. God calls me to be different than the world. I'm not better than anyone else, but I can't follow the world and follow God."

Jamie paused, then said, "At the bottom of the page it has a quote that says, 'My best friend is the one who brings out the best in me.' – Henry Ford."

Jamie closed the devotional book.

She finished her talk by saying, "Thank you for allowing me to share with you this morning. It really has been my honor."

She took her seat and Victor stood to preach. He shared about the sovereignty of God and free will of man. It was a message he faced with the recent developments in acquiring the new church property.

After the service Jamie set up a table in one of the classrooms and shared her devotional with those who wanted one. It was a good time of fellowship.

Julius saw Victor down the hall while he was in line to buy a copy of Jamie's book. He stepped out of line to speak with his pastor.

He said, "Pastor Vic, I got a letter from my dad yesterday. He wants to meet me!"

Victor said, "That's an answer to prayer Julius. When do you want to go?"

Julius answered, "I've got school and work all week and Saturday. I'm thinking about next Sunday after church. They have visitation then."

Victor asked, "Would you like me to ride over there with you?"

Julius answered, "If you can get away, I'd like it a lot."

Victor said, "No problem. We'll go over after church. I'm looking forward to it."

Julius replied, "Me too. I've waited a long time to meet my dad."

Victor's heart hurt a little for the young man.

Chapter 47

The following Sunday afternoon Victor picked Julius up at his house.

They arrived at Stonehill Maximum Security Prison and checked in at the visitor's window. As they entered, Victor could actually feel the darkness and oppression filling the facility. After a short wait, Julius was able to go into another area where he would be able to meet with his dad.

While he waited, Victor talked to one of the guards. He introduced himself and found out the guard's name was Marshall.

Victor asked, "Are there usually a lot of visitors here?"

Marshall answered, "Mostly around the holidays. Most of the guys have visitors when they first get here, but it slows down pretty quick."

Victor said, "I guess that makes sense. It's sad. I'm sure you have to be on your toes working somewhere like this."

Marshall replied, "Yes, we do. These are rough men. You can't let your guard down or you could pay a very high price."

Victor asked, "Are there any ministries serving here?"

Marshall answered, "We have a chaplain who comes by when needed. There was a church who used to have services here. I guess they gave it up about three years ago."

Victor asked, "Would it be possible for a church to have a service here if they wanted to?"

Marshall explained, "You would have to get it approved by the warden. He's usually pretty open to positive experiences for the guys in here. You have to follow the letter of the law as far as the rules go. Guys have to be background checked and searched coming and going. At least that's how it was with the last group."

Victor asked, "That sounds very reasonable. Marshall, you have a very dangerous job. Would you mind if I prayed for you?"

Marshall said, "You seem like a good man. You can pray for me. But I'm not closing my eyes."

Victor said, "I understand."

He then prayed for the prison guard and the prison.

Julius was in a visitation room. There was a row of booths with glass in front of them and phones on the right side of the wall. Julius waited for his turn and then had a seat. The guard told him to pick up the phone when his dad arrived. Julius sat there for what seemed like an eternity, but it was actually only a couple of minutes.

A large African American male in a blue tattered prison uniform walked up to the booth. He sat down. He and Julius stared at one another through the glass. Julius finally reached and picked up the phone. The prisoner did the same.

Julius said, "Thank you for meeting me. I'm Julius."

The prisoner said, "I'm Cecil. I'm glad you came to visit. I'm sorry we have to meet like this."

Julius said, "It's fine. I don't mind."

Cecil asked, "How is Wanda?"

Julius answered, "Mom? She's good. I told her I was meeting you. She was glad."

Cecil said, "That's good. She was a great woman. She deserved better from me. I was young and stupid. I didn't realize how special she was."

Julius said, "She took good care of me. She had it tough, but she's made the best of it."

Cecil said, "I know I have no right to ask this, but could you tell her I really did care for her. She was the best thing I've ever had in my life and I blew it. Tell her I'm happy she is doing well."

Julius answered, "Of course I'll tell her. I think she'll be glad to hear it."

Cecil said, "So, Julius. You're a fine looking young man. What are you doing with your life?"

Julius answered, "Like I wrote to you, I was on a bad path. God saved me and I went away to a ranch for help. I graduated high school last May and I started college in the capital city last week. It's going good."

Cecil said, "My son...a college boy. That's pretty incredible."

Julius just smiled.

Cecil asked, "What are you going to do?"

Julius answered, "I'm not sure yet. I work at a new bar-b-q joint in Westside. It's doing well. I'm considering getting my counseling degree or possibly becoming a minister. I'm just praying about it and trusting the Lord to lead me."

Cecil said, "You talk about God as much in person as you do in your letters."

Julius replied, “He's the most important thing in my life. If it wasn't for Him I would be lost and possibly dead or in...” Julius froze.

Cecil finished his sentence for him, "...or in prison."
Julius said, "Yes, sir. I'm sorry I didn't mean to..."
Cecil laughed, "You didn't mean to bring up the fact I'm in prison? Trust me, I already know. It's okay. I regret a lot of decisions I've made that led me here. I'm happy you and Wanda are doing well. Julius, I can't be much of a father to you and I know it. But hear me when I say this: I am proud of you. You're making a lot better decisions than I did at your age."
Julius said, "Yes, sir."
They were quiet for a minute then Cecil broke the silence, "The young man you asked about in your last letter. Durand Alexander."
Julius said, "Yes. Do you know him?"
Cecil answered, "Yes, he's actually in our cell block. He seems like a solid kid. I've never had any problem with him or his guys."
Julius said, "I'll explain more later, but you can tell him I'm your son. We're good. We used to hang out some when I was younger."
Cecil said, "Sure. I'll tell him. I think our time is about up. Julius, thank you for coming by. It is an honor to meet you."
Julius asked, "Would it be okay if I come back sometime?"
Cecil said, "You want to come back? Yeah. I don't have many visitors."
Julius asked, "Do you think it would be okay if I called you...Dad?"
Cecil answered, "I'd like that. I've been called a lot worse. See you next time...Son."
Julius smiled and got up and left.

Chapter 48

Fall turned to winter and New Hope Church's building was coming together. The multipurpose sanctuary could hold three hundred and fifty people. There was a food closet, job training area, and a gym. The basketball court and gym area were used for families during the week and for children and youth services.

Victor loved the idea of the church building being the place where people gathered together to worship, learn, and fellowship. A member may be playing volleyball in a league on Tuesday night and helping hand out food the next Saturday in the same building.

Everything was still on schedule to have their first official service at the new location in a little over two weeks. It would be on Christmas Sunday and everyone was excited.

Victor was meeting with Reginald, Gabriel, and Mr. Alexander at their restaurant today to discuss a possible new prison ministry.

Victor said, "You guys have hit the jackpot with this restaurant. I really appreciate you donating a portion of your profits to our church. It has helped us keep up financially with so many ministries around here."

Mr. Alexander said, "God has blessed us much more than we have blessed others. It's like they say, 'You can't out give God.'"

Reginald asked, "Are our finances still good with the church? We certainly have helped a lot of people. Elizabeth's House, the rehab program, and Westside clean-up projects aren't cheap to fund."

Victor said, "Our spending is under budget for the year. With the generous donation by Mr. Shawn Wood, our new property has a very reasonable payment. And he has gone the extra mile to line up other donors to help finance the after-school program in our current building. Our members are giving more than ever. God certainly has provided."

Gabriel said, "Our church has definitely stepped up in helping our vets and active-duty military in our community. After our incredible Fourth of July event, Colonel Spivey said he was able to connect with several people who needed help. Being able to use the church building for some meetings has been great."

Reginald added, "Several of them have joined our recovery groups too. Alcoholism and drug use are major problems we're helping many of them face."

Victor said, "Our church has grown with so many of them and their families joining us. It was an honor to baptize your friend, Matt Beard, last week, Gabriel."

Gabriel replied, "He's a great young man. I was happy to hear he acknowledged Jesus as his Savior!"

Victor said, "Your example was very influential with him, Gabriel."

Mr. Alexander said, "Speaking of people needing the Lord, how are things progressing with the prison ministry?"

Victor answered, "I just spoke with Warden Harper yesterday. He's going through all of our paperwork and background checks. He will let me know as soon as everything is set. He seems excited about us investing in these guys' lives. It's such a dark and evil place. I could actually sense the oppression when we visited. Shining God's light into the darkness is definitely needed."

Reginald said, "I'm preparing our recovery group to accept guys who get out on parole."

Mr. Alexander said, "I got another letter from Durand. He and Cecil seem to have become better acquainted. I'm praying for my boy and Cecil to become believers in Jesus."

Victor said, "Yes. Julius has continued to share God's love with his dad. They are developing a good relationship. Cecil probably won't ever get out of prison, but Julius is being faithful to connect with him."

Gabriel said, "I'm going to have to get back to the kitchen. Can we pray before I leave?"

Beginning with Reginald, each man prayed for Jesus to allow them to be the man He created them to be. Gabriel closed the time of prayer and asked God to help them to individually follow Him regardless of the cost.

After they had prayed, a lady who was sitting in a booth with her two kids came over to their table. She said, "Excuse me. I want to tell you it's been a long time since I've seen men praying like that in public. Do you go to church around here?"

Victor answered, "Yes, I'm the pastor of New Hope Church."

She said, "My husband is in prison. My kids don't have a good male role model. I think it might be time for us to find a church."

Victor said, "Here's a card with our church's address and phone number. We would love to have you and your boys visit."

She said, "Thank you so much. We'll see you there."

As she went back to her seat, a young lady who was sitting in another booth stood up and came over to them.

She said, "Excuse me. My name is Sherrie. I'm sorry to bother you, but I heard you praying and what you told that other lady."

She was nervous and shifting her weight back and forth.

Victor said, "Yes. Is there something we can do for you?"

She said, "I'm three months pregnant and my boyfriend, Chris, just got arrested. I don't have any money or anywhere to go."

She broke down in tears.

Victor and Reginald stood up and put their hands on her shoulders.

Reginald said, "Have a seat."

She sat down. Victor asked, "How can we help you? Is it money you are wanting?"

Victor knew many people on the street would cry and tell stories to get others to donate to them. He wasn't opposed to giving her some money, but he wanted to figure out how he could best help her.

She answered, "I only ate here because I had a free sandwich coupon. Honestly, I would rather have you pray for me. I don't know if God would ever want me after what I've done. But maybe if you asked He would take care of me and my baby."

Victor said, "Of course we'll pray for you. And I've got very good news for you. I know a place you can go to for help while you're pregnant. Even better than that, I want you to know God loves you and He still wants you!"

The men shared God's love with the young girl. They took her over to Elizabeth's House and introduced her to Lisa. Victor found out her boyfriend's name was Chris Young and contacted Kevin Cathey for him. It sounded like he might be a candidate for the Second Chance Ranch.

Chapter 49

On Christmas Eve, Troy pulled up to the Kingsland Bus Terminal. He had seven guys from the Second Chance Ranch, including Antonio, with him. They had earned a trip home for Christmas. Troy checked them in and said his goodbyes.

He walked over to the other side of the terminal where a bus had pulled up and was unloading. Troy double-checked the picture on his phone and walked up to a young man.

Troy said, "Chris Young?"

He replied, "Yeah, I'm Chris. Are you Troy?"

Troy answered, "Yes, I am. You've been on that bus a long time. Are you hungry?"

Chris said, "Sure. Whatever."

Troy smiled, "Follow me. You're the third young man Kevin Cathey has sent here to avoid prison. He's keeping me busy!"

Chris said, "I'm glad to be here instead of locked up. Mr. Cathey was good to me."

Troy said, "He's a good guy. The other young men Kevin has sent this way have responded well to our program."

They walked over to the diner.

Troy said, "Grab a booth. Julius Williams is from your hometown. He graduated from high school here and is now in college."

Chris said, "I've heard of him. Some people say he used to be a bad dude."

Troy exclaimed, "He's still a bad dude! But in a good way. He's a workout warrior. Amazing on the basketball court. Antonio is the other guy from Westside. He just headed home for Christmas."

Chris said, "So it's just me and you here?"

Troy laughed, "No, Chris. I'm not that crazy. There's a couple of other guys back at the ranch. They didn't get to go home for a variety of reasons. If you do what you're supposed to do here, you get rewarded. If not, you get punished. It's not easy, but it's fair."

Chris said, "Makes sense. Troy, honestly, I would rather be home with my girlfriend, but I'll do my best while I'm here."

Troy said, "Good! But talk is cheap. Chris, you have a great opportunity to become the man God created you to be. Don't waste this second chance."

New Hope Church had been approved to have their first service in Stonehill Prison on Christmas Eve. Victor, Ramone, Julius, and Mr. Alexander all checked in and followed a guard back to a windowless room.

After being searched they went through another security door and down a hall to a room with chairs set up in a circle.

Victor and the other men stood around talking to a guard. A few minutes later the security door, opposite the one they had entered, opened up. Another guard led eleven prisoners into the room. They all went immediately to their seats, except Cecil Washington who stepped over to Julius and shook his hand, and Durand who went over to talk to his dad, Mr. Alexander.

After everyone was seated Victor said, "I appreciate you being here for our first service. I'm Pastor Victor Martinez. This is Pastor Ramone, Julius, and Mr. Alexander. We are here because Jesus put it on our hearts to come and share His love with you. We are not here to judge you or condemn you. I'd like the other guys on our team to share with you why they are here today."

Each man on the team shared how God influenced his life and saved his soul.

After they had all shared, Victor said, "As you can hear from our stories, we aren't perfect. In fact, we all deserve death and eternal separation from God because we have all sinned against Him. He knew we could never be with Him because of our sin. God will not overlook sin, it must be punished. But God loved us so much that he sent His only Son to die in our place and take our punishment. God applies this forgiveness when He opens our hearts to His love, and we acknowledge our need for a Savior."

The Holy Spirit was flowing from Victor at this point and God was speaking through his words powerfully.

"I know you live in a different world than I do. But I serve the one and only God. He's omnipotent, which means He's all powerful. He isn't afraid of the darkness of this prison. He's not afraid of who you are or what you've done. He overcomes evil and replaces it with love. A love that isn't weak, but brutally fights for what is right.

"Jesus came to earth the first time to sacrifice Himself for us on a rugged old cross. He will come back one day riding on a white horse, conquering evil, and destroying His enemies.

"I want to give you the opportunity to publicly acknowledge your need for a Savior today."

Cecil Washington, Durand Alexander, and five other men acknowledged Jesus as their Savior. It was an incredible time of the Lord pouring out His power. Even one of the guards asked to speak with Victor after the inmates were taken back to their cells. He also prayed for Salvation and asked if he could come be baptized at New Hope Church.

Chapter 50

Pastor Victor Martinez looked across New Hope Church's brand new sanctuary on this Christmas Sunday morning. His wife, Maria, was sitting with Hector and Elizabeth Gonzales. Elizabeth was holding their baby, Pablo. Victor and Maria's twins were in the new nursery. Sitting on the other side of Maria were Gabriel and Sofia Lopez.

Dwayne and Theresa had just moved out into the audience from the new worship area onstage. The worship in song this morning had been glorious. They were both glad to be able to keep working in New Hope's after-school program over by the elementary school. They were sitting with Julius and his mom, Wanda. Max and Sergio were also sitting with them.

Reginald Dupree and Mr. Alexander were sitting together. The Westside Bar-B-Q and Blues restaurant they started was a huge success downtown. They were in discussions to open another location in the capital city and possibly another in the town of Lost Creek.

Lisa was sitting on the row behind Reginald. Beside her were six young girls, including Sherrie, who had met Victor and the guys at the restaurant. She was doing well at Elizabeth's House.

The sanctuary was about sixty percent full. They still had a Spanish language first service. They had plenty of room to grow and the new space was going to be utilized every day of the week in some way.

Victor said, "New Hope Church, it is an honor to stand before you today in our new church building. Although the Lord has provided us with this beautiful new property, this building is not the Church. You are the Church! And I'm proud of you. We had our first service at Stonehill Maximum Security Prison yesterday. The Lord saved eight men who publicly acknowledged Salvation in Jesus! A light shined in the darkness, and the darkness did not overcome it!"

The congregation clapped and cheered. Several "Amens" were heard.

Victor continued, "Salvation is found in the grace of God alone through faith, not by our good works. But once we are saved, God calls us to follow Him in the way we live. A faith that does not change you does not save you! The 3t Challenge has been our way of following God in our actions. Giving God our time, talents, and treasures. Your obedience to the Lord has been both inspiring and motivating. I have seen first-hand how God has grown many of you through your obedience to Him and His Word.

"I've witnessed war heroes become heroic dads and husbands; babies without hope become healthy; prisoners in a cell become eternally free. God is bigger than our dreams and more powerful than our enemies."

Victor felt the love and power of God flowing through him. After sharing the truth from God's Word a while longer, he issued an alter call and many people came forward to meet with the Lord.

Victor then prayed a powerful prayer and dismissed his church to go impact the world.

The End

Epilogue

Five years later New Hope Church is still vibrant and growing. They have multiple services throughout the week. They have planted two other churches and invest in multiple ministries. The 3t Challenge is still regularly presented and accepted.

Pastor Victor Martinez continues to pastor New Hope Church. He and Maria love investing in the people of Westside. They had another daughter. The twins are growing and doing well.

Hector and Elizabeth had another son. They have helped launch three other crisis pregnancy homes based on Elizabeth's House.

Gabriel still manages Westside Blues and Bar-B-Q and business is booming. He is active in helping veterans who are returning from war. His son, Santiago, is doing well in school and has a three-year-old little sister.

Sergio is managing a franchise of Westside Blues and Bar-B-Q in the capital city. He's married and expecting his first child soon.

Reginald began dating Lisa and they were married three years ago. He jokes about Lisa being one addiction he doesn't want to recover from. They moved into Elizabeth's House together and continue to help young ladies in need.

Mr. Alexander helps with the prison ministry and looks forward to Durand getting out of prison. Durand is studying business and preparing to work for his dad when he is released.

Cecil Williams became an outspoken Christian in prison. He passed away from heart failure about a year ago. Many men in Stonehill Maximum Security Prison were led to Christ because of Cecil.

Troy and Rachel were married by the lake at the Second Chance Ranch. They went into full-time local church ministry in another state. They have a son and daughter.

Julius Williams finished college in three years and is currently attending seminary. He is now an associate pastor in the capital city while he is finishing his degree. He has been out to Second Chance Ranch several times to speak to the students.

The current camp director at Second Chance Ranch is Antonio, who graduated college with a psychology degree. He is in his first year at the ranch, and is continuing the great work of giving people a second chance.

Max followed a path he wouldn't have imagined in his wildest dreams. But that's a story for another time.

A Note to the Reader about Salvation

I hope you enjoyed the book Second Chances. Although this a fictional book, the principles are based in truth. As pointed out several times throughout the book the 3t Challenge is about people's stewardship to God, not their Salvation. Without Salvation, the 3t Challenge is worthless.

We all need to be saved from our sins. The Bible says that every person has sinned (Romans 3:23). It goes on the say, while we don't deserve Salvation, God offers it to us as a free gift (Romans 6:23). In fact, while we were enemies of God and living in sin, God sent His only Son to die for us (Romans 5:8). God did this because He loves us so much and we can receive eternal life with God by believing in His Son Jesus Christ (John 3:16). We show evidence of this faith in Jesus by believing in our hearts and confessing with our mouths that Jesus is Lord (Romans 10:9-10).

The very first thing we're supposed to do when we are saved is to be baptized (Romans 6:4-5). The next step is fellowship with other believer's and growing spiritually.

God loves you no matter how bad you think you are. You are not too far gone for Jesus to reach out and save you. Call out to God, turn from the direction you are going and follow Him.

You can do that right now in your own words if you like. If you need someone to talk with or are interested in learning more about what it means to have a relationship with Jesus Christ, a great resource is 1-888-Need-Him (1-888-633-3446). Or on the web, go to www.needhim.org. You can also chat with someone about what a relationship with Jesus is all about at www.chataboutjesus.com. I pray you will acknowledge Jesus as your Lord and receive Salvation today!

The 3t Challenge for You

Just as Pastor Victor issued the 3t Challenge to his congregation, I would like to offer it to you. If you are a Christian, God is calling you to follow Him. The 3t Challenge is simply spending your time, talents and treasures the way the Holy Spirit leads you. Remember we aren't saved by our good works. The 3t Challenge is a practical way to follow God after we have received Salvation. Sometimes it helps to write things down to remind us of our commitments. Below is a commitment pledge you may want to sign to remind you of the Challenge you are accepting. Please pray about this and don't take this pledge lightly.

"I will, to the best of my ability, serve God with my time, talents, and treasures for the next year. I acknowledge that only the free gift of God's grace can save me. This is an expression of my desire to follow God with what He has given me. Through prayer and obeying Biblical principles I will trust God to lead me as I strive to follow Him."

____

Name

____

Date

Helping You Succeed with the 3t Challenge

How can you use your TIME more efficiently for God? What can you sacrifice to spend more of your time following Jesus?

How can you creatively use your TALENTS for the Lord? Everyone has abilities they can use for the Kingdom. What are yours?

How can you spend your TREASURES in a better way for Jesus? What are some innovative ways you can give to the Lord?

A word of encouragement for you:
God has created you just the way you are for a very special purpose that only you can fulfill. God loves you and wants you to live an abundant life. It may not always be easy to follow Him, but ultimately it will be worth it! Trials and temptations will be tough, but God is bigger and better than any obstacle you may face. Fight the good fight and keep your journey on the straight and narrow path. God loves you so much that He sent His Son to die for you.

For more information on the 3t Challenge please contact:
www.3tChallenge.com

Discussion Questions

Chp 1 When Pastor Victor looked across New Hope Church he was excited to see many new believers. When you look across your church each Sunday what do you see? Are you satisfied with what you see?

Chp 2 Julius is told that "God will bless your obedience." Has that been your experience? Can you share some of those experiences?

Chp 5 Discuss Mr. Alexander's long held anger. What are the harmful effects of harboring unresolved anger?

Chp 6 In this chapter the 3t Challenge was discussed. How are you doing with intentionally giving your time, talents, and treasure? What kind of example is your church exhibiting in their giving? What is your greatest challenge in fulfilling the 3t Challenge?

Chp 7 Pastor Victor mentioned that Jesus lived his life "on mission". What does that mean to you?

Chp 11 A time of fellowship with friends is evident here. Do you make it a priority to fellowship with friends? How important is it to your spiritual life?

Chp 13 1st Corinthians 12 teaches that the body is made up of different parts for different tasks. Have you considered your unique SHAPE? Thinking about this, what are your gifts or strengths in each of the letters of SHAPE?
S. -Spiritual Gifts. Do you know your spiritual gift?
H. -Heart. What areas do you have a heart for?
A. -Abilities. What abilities has God given you?
P. -Personality. How can you use your personality for Kingdom work?
E. -Experiences. What experiences have you gone through that can help others?

Chp 15 Pastor Victor feels he has a directive from God. Have you ever had God answer the cry of your heart? Share your experience.

Chp 16 After a series of agonizing events Maria said "our hope is not in this world". How does this statement impact you in your day to day dealing with the difficulties you face? Does your walk bear witness to this?

Chp 20 During the bus ride home Julius "reflected on the things he had learned at the ranch". Do you spend time "reflecting" on what you are learning? Discuss the value of this and the value of sharing with others what you are learning.

Chp 22 Has anyone ever laid hands on you and prayed? How did that feel? Under what circumstances do you think this should be done?

Chp 23 Did you learn how to be a good parent from your father? If not what model have you used? The bible teaches about authentic manhood. List some character traits an awesome father and husband should have.

Chp 28 & 29 After some anxious moments with her own baby Elizabeth noticed a young lady crying as she looked at her own newborn. Thinking about your own personality do you possess the trait of caring about others even in your time of need?

Chp 30 Troy shared his personal story with Julius as a word of encouragement. Have you given any thought to your own story? If not, would you think about it and share it with someone as a word of encouragement? Your testimony is a powerful tool share it as often as you can.

Chp 33 In this chapter Pastor Victor felt led by God to do something uncomfortable and odd. Have you ever felt a nudging to do something which seemed strange to you?

Chp 34 Do you believe in chance meetings where God was up to something? In this chance meeting Elizabeth met Lisa at the restaurant. God was up to something! Do you have an experience like this?

Chp 36 Pastor Victor explained the 3t Challenge and asked for testimonies about it. Have you considered the 3t Challenge? What are your feelings about it? If you have accepted the challenge, share what the results have been.

Chp 41 Reginald indicated doing God's work was not easy but it was worth it. What are you willing to do to encourage those in your church who are overloaded with ministry? Discuss ways you as an individual or a small group could encourage your Pastor.

Chp 43 Have you ever been a part of a ministry like the pregnancy crisis center which has to totally depend on God for their survival? Do you depend in God's provision for all your needs? Discuss the challenges in this lifestyle.

Chp 44 Look at Pastor Victor's prayer and think about the wording of it. What does this suggest to you about Pastor Victor? What does the rest of this chapter say about God and his provision?

Chp 47 Pastor Victor was always aware of opportunities for ministry. How observant are you to the needs around you? Is there a ministry opportunity you should be involved in right now?

Chp 48 Mr. Alexander said, "You can't out give God." What does this mean to you? What does it take to live like that? How do you start?

Chp 49 Does your church have a prison ministry? What would it take to start one? Is that something you could be involved in?

Chp 50 Pastor Victor said that the new building was not the church. The people are. Do you live your way that would inspire others to pursue a relationship with God? Is there anything that needs to change in you?

44278521R10101

Made in the USA
Charleston, SC
22 July 2015